The House at Pritchard Place

A New Orleans Paranormal Mystery

by
Evelyn Klebert

The House at Pritchard Place
A New Orleans Paranormal Mystery
By Evelyn Klebert

A Cornerstone Book
Published by Cornerstone Book Publishers

Fourth Cornerstone edition 2026

Cornerstone Book Publishers
Hot Springs Village, AR
www.cornerstonepublishers.com

ISBN 978-1-61342-292-2

Dedication

For My Family,
Michael, Robert, Jonathan, and Corey,
Who Always Keep Me Steady and on Course,
When I Lose My Way

Table of Contents

The House at Pritchard Place

A New Orleans Paranormal Mystery

THE ROCKING CHAIR

1

It was different when they shared a room. Things didn't seem to happen quite as much when she had her sister asleep not far away. But as it was, at thirteen, Cassandra Ashford felt that she was too old to share close quarters with her younger sister Elise, who then was only ten. At the time, it didn't really bother Elise. In many ways, she was a pragmatist, and the idea of spreading her treasures more decoratively throughout the room's square footage did appeal to her. And it wasn't outside the realm of possibility that when Cassie vacated, Elise might finally be able to convince her mother to buy her a rocking chair. In the past, she'd made the request more than once, and it had fallen with a resounding thud on deaf ears. After all, it was a rather bizarre ask for a little girl. "Wouldn't you rather have a nice dollhouse?" Or, in Elise's case, they'd even offered her a train set. She did have a bit of a tomboy aspect to her personality. But no, she was set on a rocking chair. So, her lovely mother had smiled warmly and in a placating tone informed her that there simply wasn't enough space in the girls' bedroom.

Well, now that Cassie was moving out into the former sewing room across the hall, that argument wouldn't hold water anymore. And Mrs. Lavender would so enjoy a rocking chair. Of course, Elise knew that wasn't her real name, but she seemed quite complacent in allowing Elise to call her that. In truth, they hadn't really been on any sort of speaking terms until about a year ago.

Elise was relatively young when they first moved into the house at Pritchard Place, just three. And as long as she could remember, she would catch glimpses of the old woman with the ivory-colored cane and long lavender shawl lurking around the house. For a time, Elise just assumed she lived there with them. Then, on her fifth birthday, she mentioned Mrs. Lavender and realized disturbingly that everyone thought she'd made her up. The lady that she saw often with the long crocheted lavender shawl, everyone assumed Elise had imaginatively created. And then, it became the running joke in the house: "Did you see Mrs. Lavender today, Elise?" or "Did Mrs. Lavender help you pick out your school clothes?" Her father had deemed the old woman her imaginary friend, and everyone else followed suit. Except, of course, Cassie, Cassie believed her, although Elise didn't confide much in her. It wasn't her way. So, she simply stopped mentioning her, but Mrs. Lavender didn't go away.

Sometimes she'd wake up at night and find the old lady softly patting her hand. Elise knew very well that the old woman was sad. She could feel it, although with determination she blocked that aspect out. After all, there was only so much a young girl could handle. She had her own worries growing up and all. And then, after a very long time, Mrs. Lavender started communicating, sort of mumbling at first as though she was talking to herself. Seems she'd lost some children in that very house, three to be exact — scarlet fever or was it yellow fever? Elise couldn't be sure, and then the lady had died herself. Although now, she was somewhat confused and kept looking for her kids. It was a bit much for a nine-year-old to take on. But

Elise, being an exceptionally smart girl, tried her best. She tried to coax Mrs. Lavender to move on and go into the light to be reunited with her lost children. But as deaf as her parents' ears seemed to be concerning some things, it was nothing compared to this woman. She simply would ignore Elise completely and start mumbling her antiquated lullabies. It was at that point that Elise learned what she deemed one of the more important lessons in life: *"Nothing before its time,"* or more succinctly, *"Everything has a time."* At any rate, Mrs. Lavender wasn't going to budge until she was good and ready. But it was a fact that the elderly lady did always seem to be looking around for a good place to sit. She seemed to think if she could just rock in her "rocking chair" and sing her lullabies, maybe her lost children would find their way back to her. Elise very much doubted that things would turn out the way the old woman hoped, but she could try to make her more comfortable.

Thus, the rocking chair. Tenth birthday: "What would you like for your birthday Elise?"

"A rocking chair."

Wrinkled nose, her mother had a lovely little sharp nose that she tended to wrinkle when she was displeased. "Wouldn't you rather some toys, dolls, or, well, more trains?"

Eleventh birthday: "What would you like for your birthday Elise?"

"A rocking chair."

Wrinkled nose, plus the frown, was not at all a good sign. "How about a new bicycle, a pink one?"

"Purple, I can't stand pink."

Twelfth birthday, "What would you like for your birthday Elise?"

"A rocking chair."

More wrinkling and frowning, "Wouldn't you—"

"No, nothing but the rocking chair! That's all I want!"

"But—"

"Don't you want me happy? It's my birthday," feigned hysterics, which truly chafed against the grain of her somewhat pragmatic and, at times, stoic nature. After all, if she wasn't a tad detached, how could she deal with, well, all she seemed to have to deal with constantly?

"Now, don't cry, Elise."

She wasn't really crying, just pretending to, in fact, having a time working up any semblance of fake tears, although she did manage to put her index finger in one eye, and it was tearing up and hurting more than a bit. She dearly hoped Mrs. Lavender would appreciate the lengths she was going to for her. "I just," sob, sob, "want," gurgle snort, "a rocking chair, nothing else."

Her mother was still frowning but did put her arms around her. After all, she wasn't a block of ice. And that birthday, Elise got a lovely white rocker for her room and little else. And truth be told, she'd had her eye on a lovely model train kit to add to her collection. But Mrs. Lavender did seem pleased, although she grumbled a bit about the chair not being the best fit for her. But Elise would often find her rocking in the chair and murmuring her lullabies to her lost children. Then when Elise was fourteen, Mrs. Lavender stopped visiting her and stopped rocking in the chair. Elise felt that the time had arrived, and her children might have just shown up to lead her where she needed to go. She was happy for her but would miss her more than she liked to admit. It had been a comfort having her around, particularly reassuring to have an ally when she had begun seeing everything else.

♦

"And no one has seen him."

"Really? No one at all?"

"Well, I don't know if no one. But no one I know. I asked Adele, you know, Adele Caswell. She lives directly across the street from the old Warrick house and said she hasn't seen the new owner. But he has two rather over-sized German shepherds patrolling the yard."

"Hmm, but isn't Adele Caswell out quite a bit? She owns—"

"Yes, yes, The Flower Stop on the corner of Zimpel and Joliet St., poor dear works all the time. She lost two of her best employees. Young people back to college for the fall couldn't even wait until she replaced them. Young people these days. No sense of responsibility."

She nodded, delicately sipping her hot cup of peppermint tea so that it didn't scorch her lips. "So, Adele being out so much, may have just missed Mr.—mmm, what did you say his name was again, Martha?"

The elderly lady wrinkled her nose a bit, trying to recall. And at that moment, Elise was again struck at her resemblance to her late mother, at least when vexed. "Oh dear, what was it again? Peculiar name, McCaully? No, that wasn't it. McMurty? No, no, he's the fellow that writes westerns."

Elise smiled softly, "Did you say Mcginvale?"

Martha's features became quite animated. "That's it, Elise, Mcginvale, John, no, no, Joseph maybe. Mcginvale, what does that make him Irish or something, Elise?"

"Hard to say, Martha," she commented. She heard a rumble over their heads and noted that some dark menacing-looking clouds had rolled in directly over Martha Densford's lovely white, wooden lattice patio cover. No doubt, it would cut short their Saturday morning tea and gab session that had become somewhat of a routine for her and Elise. Martha lived in a lovely cream-colored house right on the corner of Freret and Cambronne St. that oddly enough had a huge cobble-stoned patio right out in the front yard, surrounded by a white picket fence. Martha was Elise's senior by about thirty-five years, but Elise did enjoy spending time with the elderly white-haired lady, who had quite a grasp on the history of New Orleans. Unfortunately, these days, she only seemed interested in gossip about the residents of this several-block area of streets near the Riverbend section of New Orleans where they lived.

"Well, I find it odd that no one has seen the man." Elise smiled. Martha was eccentric in her way, actually in many ways, and tended to hang onto an idea once she got her fingernails into it.

Elise glanced up again in response to the low rumbling overhead. She supposed she should warn Martha and cut this tête-à-tête short, but on a level, she had to admit that she was interested. The Warrick house, quite a huge sprawling sort of place, was a curiosity to her. She'd never actually stepped foot in it. The residents, and as far as she'd known, there had always been one sort of Warrick there or another, had been a bit on the reclusive side. Although the Warrick family, who owned it recently, cousins of the original Warricks, had built a lovely little tree house in one of the great oaks on the property. And there had been children, and they'd waved and smiled at Elise as she strolled down the street on one of her late afternoon walks. But the place undeniably had a strange vibe, not bad exactly, but surely complicated.

"I'm surprised the house passed out of the Warrick hands," Elise commented almost to herself. "So, you say he doesn't have a family."

Martha nodded, "Yes, that's what — now, who told me that? Oh yes, Cora, Cora Moran. You know, lovely girl, just a bit younger than you Elise, lives up on Dublin St. but was out walking with her two girls, twins, you know. I think they're about ten now. Well, I was sitting here just about a week ago, and she stopped, and we got to talking. She said he isn't married and has to be middle-aged, maybe late forties, maybe fifties, but a nice-looking man. Apparently, he was moving in, and she welcomed him to the neighborhood. She said he was pleasant but didn't seem to want to spend a lot of time talking."

Elise sipped her tea to stop from commenting about the *"no one has seen him"* supposition. "You must admit that's a large house for one person."

Martha's eyes narrowed a bit. "That is exactly what I was thinking, Elise. What exactly will he do rattling around that huge place all alone? I guess those big dogs could keep him company, giant German shepherds. Did I tell you that?"

Elise smiled and nodded, feeling the slightest spray of a rain shower beginning to fall from overhead.

The Old Warrick House

2

E lise slowly walked back up Freret St. The shower threatening to douse her and Martha's Saturday morning tea had
diminished once she'd said her goodbyes. The sky was still
rumbling overhead, and an occasional raindrop grazed the top of
her hair. It was just as well that she did not have to return home
right away, as Elise was deeply lost in thought. There were so
many thoughts that she kept wandering several blocks in the
other direction down Dante St, straight down to the old Warrick
house and the man who had now taken possession of it.

She frowned to herself. Elise certainly didn't consider herself
a gossip, but she wasn't beyond indulging in others' gossip to
gain information. And it was Saturday, her day off from her work
as a part-time archivist at The New Orleans Historic Collection
down on Royal St. in the French Quarter. It was a job that she'd
held for over fifteen years, and she enjoyed it — enjoyed putting
together collections, researching, and categorizing old docu-
ments. But lately, she sighed deeply. Well, nothing extraordinary
had happened.

She stopped walking and glanced back up at the sky. The
storm could pass over, or it could rain cats and dogs. It was pretty

much a toss-up, or as she preferred to look at it, a gamble. The truth was she was bored. She was itching for something interesting to happen, so she spun around and headed back down Freret St. toward Dante St. She headed toward Dante St. and the old Warrick house, where she just might find something interesting.

She was due for Sunday supper at Cassie's house tonight, and many things needed her attention before she headed over there. But nothing that particularly intrigued her, nothing that pulled her like Martha's suppositions about the new owner of the Warrick House. Not that she gave much credit to her assertions about the mysterious nature of the new owner, but Elise did have to admit there were a few facts that lay enmeshed in Martha's rambling accounts. Joseph Mcginvale had moved into that sprawling house. She hesitated to call it a mansion, though it did have more acreage and square feet than any other structure in a several-block radius. He did have two large dogs on the property. While that could simply be his personal liking for certain breeds of dogs, it could also be an effort to discourage anyone from approaching the residence.

And on top of all of that, Elise was restless. She'd felt a restlessness in her skin ever since she'd returned from her trip to Southern France nearly six months before. It had ignited something within her, something that she hadn't been able to quite put her finger on, like that nagging little feeling that you aren't quite doing what you're supposed to be doing. As her feet continued to meander down Dante St., she mused that she might be heading into the Underworld as in *Dante's Inferno.* She distractedly wondered if it were possible for people to become so dissatisfied that they sought out danger, actually actively craved it.

And then she stopped, hearing the sky rumbling overhead with a threatening reminder that the storm might not be over, not over at all, but just beginning.

Staring at the wrought iron gate and metal fence surrounding the property, she remembered now why she seldom traveled in this direction. There was undeniably something about the Warrick House that felt, well, tragic. And then she crossed the street.

♦

When Mrs. Lavender left, Elise was of mixed feelings on the subject. On the one hand, she was more than pleased that the unhappy lady had moved on to hopefully find solace in a more pleasant afterlife than her earthly existence had been. But on the other hand, Elise was left behind with Mrs. Lavender's white rocking chair that, in truth, she didn't care for in the least. However, she did occasionally muse about painting it an eye-popping orange or a psychedelic purple. Beyond the problem with the chair, which in the big scheme of things was minor, there were the other things. There were things that Elise had the sneaking suspicion that Mrs. Lavender's presence had somehow held at bay.

Suffice to say, there were bugs at Pritchard Place. They were not bugs that one could easily rid oneself of with a can of spray but rather bugs that not everyone could see. They were nasty, oversized bugs, which it became more than clear that only she was aware of.

"Did you see that?"

Cassie looked up from a magazine she'd been reading, somewhat bleary-eyed. "See what?"

"Behind you, on the wall, I think it was a roach."

Of course, Cassie jumped up out of her chair, practically leaping across the den. "What! Where, where did you see it?"

And then, not unexpectedly, a massive hunt took place in the room, ending with her mother declaring that it had left or Elise had likely made an error.

But she hadn't, and she saw it again, big as life in her room. Actually, it was in the middle of the night. She thought she'd been dreaming when she woke up and saw it slowly scurrying around on the ceiling of her room. She considered screaming, but there was an analytical side to Elise's nature that had come in quite handy when such things occurred. And in her fourteen years of life, unexpected, unusual things had occurred more often than one might expect.

So, she lay back in the bed and watched it, unsure now that it was a roach because it didn't act like a regular roach. It was scurrying in circles, and the more she observed it, the more she saw that the thing was shifting colors — from black to reddish in the middle to a weird sort of orange glow around it. And Elise, watching it so closely, began to feel odd, irritated, as though it undeniably was giving off a really bad feeling.

She found herself angry, contemplating throwing a shoe at it. And the more she became upset, the bigger its middle seemed to be until suddenly another bug popped out from inside it — just like it, but of course smaller.

She felt vexed. What was this in her room? And then, in her infinite wisdom, she told herself to be calm, calm, and not upset. It took a little while, perhaps twenty minutes, perhaps half an hour of watching the bugs scuttling around. But in time, they lost some of their ugly orange glow and, dare she say, seemed to shrink a little. Then finally, they left, didn't just disappear but ran out the doorway, still clinging to the ceiling. So, they weren't gone. They just had vacated her room.

◆

She stood across the street from the old Warrick house as it was popularly known as in the small neighborhood. And Elise remembered why she didn't travel down this way often. It was an unusual house for the area, larger than most, but not all, particularly as one got closer to Carrollton Avenue. She had to admit some of the houses on that street did rival those mansions on St. Charles Avenue. But back here, around these few blocks comprised of Zimpel, Freret, Burthe, Joliet, Cambronne, Dante, and Dublin Streets, the homes, while largely individual, were predominately wood framed doubles, shotguns, and camelbacks with an occasional exception of a one-story rambling ranch style like that of Martha Densford. The old Warrick house, though, was unusual with its privacy fence, a large brown wood wrapping around its acreage. From what she could see, large oak trees, magnolias, and possibly pines stretched above the fence that was not so high that travelers could not gaze over the top through its partitions.

It was not exactly what she would call a formal house, large yes, but a sort of grayish wood, three columns supporting an upper story porch and several layers of brick steps leading down into the long walkway. And the main structure was flanked on the sides by several supporting wings. She didn't know if the house had been added onto at some point. And she had no idea how old it was, but something told her it was—at least a century.

The sky overhead rumbled, but Elise crossed the street to the cement sidewalk directly in front of the structure. It was undeniable that the atmosphere thickened as she moved closer to it. There was a heaviness, a density in the air, although the impending storm lent some natural atmospheric humidity to the equation. But Elise was sure that she was feeling something else. It was sort of like moving through an emotional molasses. This was the closest description she could provide.

She stood in front of the high wrought iron gate blocking her entrance onto the property. The monstrously sized German shepherds that Martha had described were nowhere to be seen. Breathing deeply, she let her eyes wander to wherever they were drawn. It wasn't exactly a "bad" feeling per se that she was getting from the house, but dulling somehow, indeed, as though there was an odd sort of energy at work here.

New Orleans, she'd found, was a complicated city. It was filled with so many different manners of existence, on both the earthly plane and on a more psychic one. There were so many divergent phenomena, in fact, that many she simply ignored. She did not take the time to seek them out. And she was wondering, in the moment, if perhaps she should do that very thing with the old Warrick House — walk away, leave its mysteries to itself.

But just at that very instant, that particular decision was taken out of her hands as the heavy front door on the front of the abode swung open. And her eyes took in the full appearance of that very mysterious gentleman that Martha Densford had sworn so few had seen.

He stepped out onto the porch. In response, Elise took a step backward but found that the back of her foot was already on the edge of the street.

The tall man hesitated momentarily, focusing on her, she was certain, and then proceeded to wave. "Well, hello there," he said in an almost clipped English accent.

Elise frowned. No one had said the fellow was English. She thought to quickly walk away from this very awkward situation. But she didn't. She stood there somewhat rooted to the spot.

In several quick strides, he was on the other side of the wrought iron gate, which actually came only up to her neck. "So, are you a neighbor?" he said rather jovially.

She forced a smile. "No, not really, just a passerby."

He was a smiling, tall, slim, clean-shaven dark-haired man with hair just graying. "Ah, so you don't live around here?"

"Well, not on Dante St., actually over on Freret."

"So, that's not really far?"

"No, I was just out taking a stroll."

He nodded, still smiling but looking her over a bit. "Well, I've just moved in, haven't met many of the neighbors."

"Yes, well, it's a lovely area. I'm sure you will enjoy it."

"Joseph Mcginvale."

She waited. Damn, there was no way around this. "Elise Ashford."

"Well, Ms. Ashford, as it seems that it will be raining rather soon. How would you like a cup of tea in my sunroom?"

She felt a little jolted. This certainly was unanticipated. "Um, well." It was rather ridiculous for her even to contemplate going into a stranger's house. After all, how many murders begin in such a manner? But there was a part of her, a rebellious part, that wanted to see the inside of that house. And there might never be another opportunity.

"I see you're hesitant. Understandable, but I assure you all my intentions are quite honorable."

She smiled, feeling tired, reckless, and with a few drops of rain falling on her shoulder. "Well, maybe for just a cup of tea, Mr. Mcginvale." And then he smiled and swung open the gate.

Joseph McGinvale

⸛

3

"*Now don't talk to strangers and never, never go off with someone you don't really know.*"

The advice she'd given to her sister Cassie's young children now resounded in her mind, echoing off the slippery walls of her judgment. Did this make her a hypocrite? She wondered.

Of course, Joseph Mcginvale did not set off any readily apparent alarms in her. And usually, she was pretty good at estimating danger in all its various guises. As she'd noted, he was tall, perhaps just a bit shorter than her niece Caroline's Max Gravier. He was dressed more or less casually, perhaps casually for a Brit — nice dark brown trousers and a pullover, beige sweater. Nothing stood out in his features, a bit bland in her estimation, making him fall just short of handsome, though, in truth, there wasn't anything particularly lacking in that regard. Perhaps it was Elise's peculiar sensibility that found him falling short. Her estimation of what she found attractive in the opposite sex often had much more to do with personality than physically benevolent features. His face lay more on the less chiseled side, she thought, not what she'd call a strong chin. The one thing she might say about his appearance, which she found of interest, was that his eyes seemed alert, a dark brown to nearly black shade, not large eyes, but attentive to everything. It wasn't precisely that he seemed benign, more so that he didn't scream lunatic or serial killer to her psychic awareness.

All of that aside, there was still the house. As she stepped across the threshold onto its wooden floor, she glanced about the rather large room that she interpreted as some sort of a den, though it was empty, completely devoid of furniture. "Oh, sorry about the sparseness of the place. I'm expecting another moving truck with the balance of my furniture from Connecticut sometime next week," he explained smoothly.

Barely acknowledging what he'd said, Elise stepped further into the light-filled room, trying to absorb as much as she could quickly. After all, she had no intention of staying here for long. "Connecticut? I just assumed you were from overseas," she remarked a bit absently. The room was huge, like two parlors connected in the old days. The walls were a lovely warm beige shade, and a quaint little staircase with a black wrought iron railing just to the left of the front door. Beyond that, there was a fireplace with a creamy wooden mantle across the great expanse, several interior columns to break the space of the large room, and a bar connecting toward possibly an open kitchen, she suspected. Not what she'd expected from the outside, which had suggested a more closed-in protected sort of space.

"Ah yes, the accent, I am originally from Manchester but have lived in the States for almost twenty years."

"You must miss home," she murmured, glancing around with distraction, still feeling various unidentified pulls around her.

"Occasionally," he said, and then she noticed suddenly he was watching her quite closely. "Do you like the house?" he said, with a tinge of curiosity.

No doubt he'd picked up the intense way she was canvassing things. She smiled, trying to be affable, although granted, it wasn't her strong suit. "It seems very nice."

He nodded, "Well, the sunroom is this way, just through the kitchen."

They passed through the light-filled kitchen, painted a pale yellow color that made her feel rather indifferent, into the small sunroom on the east side of the house. She'd noted the various dishes and kitchen apparatuses already decorating the space. Evidently, living room furniture, he could do without but not cooking paraphernalia.

There was a glass table in the bright sunroom, which looked out on a back patio, and a small pool empty of water. "Do you swim?" she asked a bit abruptly.

He glanced at the pool, frowning a bit. "Well, not much these days. I haven't decided what to do with that."

She sat in one of the black wooden chairs, "It's wonderful exercise if you can find someone to take care of it for you. Especially in this area of the country, it takes quite a bit of effort to keep the algae blooms under control."

He laughed with a deep laugh that made Elise notice for the first time that Mr. Joseph Mcginvale's eyes were indeed brown, perhaps not quite as dark as she'd formerly surmised. "You don't mind if I just put the tea kettle on?"

"Tea kettle? Really? Most people have given that over in favor of a microwave."

"Well, Elise," and she noted that he'd taken to using her first name. "I'm someone who doesn't believe all the old ways are entirely without value."

♦

She checked her watch. It was approaching noon, and she was still sitting in the sunroom of the old Warrick house, sipping a cup of warm Earl Grey tea with the mysterious Joseph Mcginvale. She suspected that if Martha Densford got wind of this, Elise would become the apex of a whole new swirl of gossip.

"So, I take it you like the house."

"Well, that would be a pity if I didn't," he said a little too quickly, which made her wonder about the veracity of what he was saying. But then again, she was of a suspicious nature. "It is quite comfortable and airy."

"But large, I mean for one person. Do you have family that will be joining you?"

"No, no, I was married a long time ago, but no children."

"Ah, I see," she commented, sipping her tea.

"And are you married, Elise?"

"No."

"Ever been married?"

"No," she stated flatly.

"Hmm," he said, then sipped his tea. She wondered with a little irritation what that meant, so she asked.

"What does that mean?"

"I'm sorry?"

"You know, the hmmm noise."

He awkwardly laughed, "Oh, I didn't mean to offend you. I just thought it odd that you've never been married."

"Why is that?" she asked pointedly.

"Because you're such a lovely woman, I imagine you've had many suitors."

She relaxed a bit at the compliment, not nearly as affronted now. "Well, people choose not to marry for many reasons."

"Of course, like what exactly?"

She smiled, "Now that would be none of your business. So, what did you say you did?"

"Ah, I'm a researcher, a historical researcher." He seemed to respond rather amiably to her quick shift in subject.

"Really? How fascinating, are you published?"

"Yes, mostly in journals," he murmured, and again she detected something elusive in his response.

"That does sound interesting."

"And you?"

"Me?"

Joseph smiled at her with interest. He seemed only encouraged by her prickliness. "Do you work?"

"Oh yes, I'm an archivist."

"A researcher and an archivist. Sounds like ours was a fortuitous meeting."

She sipped her tea. It had cooled enough to make it somewhat palatable now. "Do you think so?"

Another smile, he found her amusing. And she wondered if it was time to leave. "So, where do you work, Elise, as an archivist?"

"The Historic New Orleans Collection."

"Oh, in the French Quarter." Damn, she'd certainly given out more information than she'd intended.

"Well, you must have transported much of your research here. I mean books and papers."

"Yes, most."

"Because as you said, the furniture is still coming."

He nodded, "Perceptive, yes, the rooms upstairs are filled with boxes."

"That seems quite natural. People prioritize whatever is of most value to them."

"Indeed, Elise, I suppose they do."

She smiled, feeling a slight frisson in the air as though again she had stumbled across something a bit sensitive. "Well, this has been lovely, Mr—"

"Joseph."

She nodded, rising, "Of course, but I must be going."

He followed, placing his cup on the table and standing beside her. "Well, at least now I can count you as one acquaintance I have in the neighborhood. Freret St., wasn't it?"

"Yes, yes, it is."

♦

The sky overhead had begun to clear as she began her trek back to Freret St. Elise couldn't quite shake that peculiar sensation of, well, dissatisfaction. The house, at least what she'd seen inside of the old Warrick House, had felt quite lovely. And that in itself didn't add up. She had always felt an ambiguity as she'd passed the structure in the past, an indefinable quality that told her succinctly that there was more there than met the eye. But the fact that within, she'd really seen nothing did seem somehow problematic.

And on top of that, there was this new owner, this historical researcher. Who invites a total stranger into their house for tea? How bizarre was that? She supposed he could be painfully lonely, but nothing in his manner, bearing, or dare she say, his energy spoke of such a state. And she wasn't self-indulgent enough to believe he was so captivated with her at first sight that he had to get to know her, please. Elise was forty-five, well past her femme fatale prime, although it had never been much in her nature to be a femme fatale.

So, what was going on there? Perhaps there was something else on the Warrick estate that she hadn't seen yet.

♦

He watched her from the front window as she walked away from the house. Elise Ashford was a lovely woman, petite, brunette, with very intense green eyes, and rather angular, sharp features, though undeniably it felt at times that she might shred you with her caustic nature. The man who called himself Joseph Mcginvale certainly felt curious, but clearly, not as curious as Elise Ashford was about his house. It was more than evident to him that despite his charming nature, the lady had been much more interested in the walls around him. But that truly wasn't something he felt was a problem at all. In fact, it could prove to be quite useful.

A Family Gathering

4

"S o, this Joseph Mcginvale, you thought was problematic?"

She wrinkled her nose a bit and wondered for not the first time if she was beginning to pick up traits of her mother. "No, well, I'm not sure."

"Then the house, what did you call it?"

"The Warrick House."

"Oh, that's right. You think the house is a problem?"

"Well," she considered carefully because Elise did pride herself on being factual and even-minded, not allowing herself to be carried away by emotional flurries of enthusiasm. "Originally, that's what I thought, but when I was inside with Joseph—"

"Joseph?"

"Yes, the new owner. I told you, Joseph Mcginvale."

"Yes, so you did." Cassie smiled a bit and took another sip of her coffee. Elise had arrived early at her sister's Prytania St. mansion, around four, before Cassie's family gathering to just hash things out a bit. It was true that she didn't share everything with her older sister, but she did find it helpful to bounce ideas and impressions off of her from time to time. And the truth was that outside of Cassie and her Breslin brood, there were only a handful of people she knew who were open to understanding the world as she experienced it. "Then what exactly is the problem, Elise? I mean, if the owner seems all right, and the house seems clear."

"I only saw the downstairs," she muttered with a tad of aggravation, not aggravation at Cassie but herself — for not being able to put her finger on what the real problem might be.

Cassie's usually warm, sky-blue eyes hardened as she frowned. "You know, I am a bit surprised you went in at all. After all, you don't know this fellow and terrible things happen in the world every day and, unfortunately, in this city."

Elise sipped her coffee. It was too weak. Elise preferred her coffee to be stronger and with more of a bitter bite. "Yes, I know, but something undeniably drew me."

"This man?"

Now it was her turn to frown, "You know, it's not always about a man Cassie. Just because you've been keeping company with your investigator fellow doesn't mean I have to follow suit."

"I thought you liked Peter, and I'm not keeping company with him. We really need to get you out more. That sounds so archaic, Elise."

She grimaced, wondering if she was wrinkling her nose again like her mother did when she was displeased. "I get out all the time."

"Yes, I don't just mean that block of streets around Freret St. Why don't you move in here? We have plenty of room. And I have the feeling Caroline will be leaving before too long."

"Going off somewhere with Max?" she murmured.

"No, I mean, she hasn't said that. They seem to be taking their time. I just don't like the thought of you living alone."

She smiled indulgently, "Sweet of you, Cassie, but you know I am a solitary creature, and I like my little shotgun house on Freret. It suits me."

Cassie smiled a little sadly as though she wasn't entirely convinced. "Well, I've known you long enough to know not to push you. So, what do you think is bothering you so much?"

Elise shook her head, "I wish I knew. Just something, something is nagging at me."

◆

Elise kept herself removed. She learned long ago that it was easier for her to exist in the world this way. *"I thought it odd that you've never been married."* Joseph Mcginvale's assessment of her, and one that strangely enough she'd heard more than once over her forty-five years on the earth.

Cassie, on the eve of her first marriage to Allen Breslin: *"Why don't you get married, Elise? You're so dynamic and lovely. So many men would be happy to be with you."*

Her mother, during her protracted battle with cancer at a relatively young age: *"I'd like to see you married Elise. So you wouldn't be alone."*

But what most people didn't understand was that she was rarely alone. And she saw too much and knew too much of others to consider letting anyone too close to her. Somehow it was just simpler being on her own. Did she regret it? She rarely allowed herself to consider it much. She didn't like to waste her energy on topics that were frankly non-productive.

"So, Aunt Elise, what's the news about this haunted house in your neighborhood?" Jared Breslin, Cassie's youngest, blond like his mother, just shy of twenty, interjected abruptly into the conversation. He'd torn off a huge chunk of French bread, one that Elise suspected he would soon attempt to dunk into the steaming bowl of seafood gumbo that Cassie had prepared.

"I never said it was haunted," Cassie protested.

"I haven't heard anything about this, Aunt Elise," Caroline jumped in. Caroline, Cassie's oldest child, had just turned twenty-six but had darker hair and, to her credit Elise's piercing green eyes.

Elise glanced around at all the faces seated at Cassie's huge dining room table, now looking at her eagerly for clarification. The occupants had expanded somewhat since the early days when she was actively helping Cassie raise Caroline and Jared after their father had died. Seated next to Caroline was Max Gravier, quite a solid fellow who Elise had discerned long ago was madly in love with her niece, and on one side of Cassie was their newest addition, Peter Norfleet, whom Elise could not fail to notice was becoming more and more smitten with her sister. Young Jared, just getting his feet wet in college, was still quite unattached, and she, Elise, well, was as she'd always been.

"I can't say that it's haunted. I mean, I can't say that it's not. I only got a quick look at the downstairs."

"But you felt something?" Max quizzed. Elise's eyes rested on her niece's boyfriend. She had to say Max was a formidable psychic and had proved it on more than one occasion.

She nodded with a quick smile. "Yes, my instincts tell me something is going on at the old Warrick House."

"And you went inside. How did that happen, Aunt Elise?"

She glanced over at Cassie, who had let her eyes drop surreptitiously down to her bowl of gumbo. "Well, actually, I was passing by, and the owner invited me in for tea."

Caroline's eyes widened a bit. "A woman?"

She shook her head. "No, no, a man, Joseph Mcginvale, you know he's British, originally from Manchester. Has quite the accent."

"So, how does everyone like the gumbo?" Cassie asked, clearly trying to shift the subject."

"Does he have a family?" Caroline inquired, continuing to laser beam in on Elise.

Elise sipped her iced tea, wondering exactly where Caroline was headed but not being too concerned about it. "No, he doesn't. And I thought that odd, a big place for a single man."

Caroline furrowed her brow a bit. "And he invited you in for tea?"

"Yes, yes, he did. He's some sort of historical researcher, has the whole neighborhood abuzz."

Caroline stared at her oddly, "Hmmm," she murmured, making Elise vaguely curious as to what her "hmmm" meant.

"Well, Cassie, I must say the gumbo is excellent," Peter Norfleet offered into the awkward gaping pause.

"And will you be seeing him again?" Caroline injected rather abruptly. She had to admit that from time to time, her niece did remind her of a bloodhound.

"Well, I have no idea," Elise answered with little emotion.

PARASITES

5

Usually, it would proceed like this. She'd awake invariably around 3:00 AM because there was definitely something about that time of night or rather time of the morning when things seemed active, for lack of a better word.

And they were always troublesome, those dreams, especially the in-between ones. Though, they did seem to come part and parcel with the other gifts that life had imparted her with. And when she was a girl, living alone in that bedroom on Pritchard Place, such dreams tended to get out of control.

On one particular night, she awoke and sat up in her bed. Across the room, she could see the shadows of her closet, but they weren't still as shadows ought to be. Instead, they were moving about.

"What do you want?" whispering aloud. While that might seem an odd thing to say for some, Elise had experienced enough bizarre manifestations to find it warranted.

But there was no answer, just an escalation of movement — the light flickering in and out of the open closet and a strange rustling noise. Then startlingly, she remembered quite clearly that she was a diligent girl and never left that door of her closet open.

Of course, she thought to scream, which would indeed pierce the veil of this altered state she'd awoken into. But Elise wasn't one who liked to scream. Cassie, on the other hand, was different. She would scream a lot — for bugs, for mice, for people tapping her on the shoulder unexpectedly. Probably why she never would see the things Elise did. She'd be a basket case by now if she had.

So, Elise waited and watched and tried to stay calm, not panic. She'd seen things before, and then they'd just sort of drift away eventually. There was definitely a distortion, a sort of fog mixed in with the shifting light and shadows, but every once in a while, she would see a glimpse of something disturbing — long and prickly-looking, like an extended sort of limb, although not a human one. And it did make her breath hitch up a bit, painfully in her throat. After all, she was only twelve.

"What do you want?" whispering again into the darkness, and the rustling seemed to stop for a moment as if in response. She didn't know if this was a good sign or not. But then there was dragging, a wriggling movement out of the shadows, closer to her. It was so close that she could feel a heated sensation as though some sort of flesh were next to her. She'd backed up as far against the wall as she could. But it didn't help, and it didn't stop what happened next. A face peered at her out of the dimness of the room, a face at least as big as hers but not at all human. It was some kind of an insect with many bug-like eyes over its head.

She gasped and might have screamed then. She wasn't sure because then she felt her mother's hands on her.

"Elise, Elise, wake up, dear."

She sat up in the bed, facing her mother and staring across the room. Closet closed, just silence, "Were you dreaming about something?" she asked.

She could feel her heart in her chest still pounding wildly from fear. "Yes," answering. "I was dreaming about monsters."

♦

Actually, better said, creatures from another dimension, ones not readily seen by the eyes, or so she came to understand from extensive research that she would do as she got older. As things got more complicated in her life, she would seize upon every book concerning parapsychology, psychic phenomena, ghosts, hauntings, and pretty much anything she could find. Then, when she went to college, she joined groups, heard lectures, and continued her learning so that she could deal with the world she was experiencing with a firmer grip.

And the extra knowledge certainly didn't hurt when Cassie and her children began manifesting their own psychic gifts. So, she could share some of this with them, some but never everything.

"These creatures that you see, many are parasites living off the energy of those on this plane of existence. Most people aren't even aware of them, and then others feel them in the form of negative feelings, irritation. Of course, there are positive ones, but they tend to gravitate to higher planes."

She'd had this conversation with a teacher from India who taught a class on parapsychology one summer at Loyola. She was a lovely woman, and they'd spent many hours discussing some of Elise's concerns. These were conversations she rarely felt comfortable having with anyone. But she and Dr. Rajun held a rapport that she found immensely helpful.

"But I've seen massive ones, creatures, in the past."

"Yes, they vary in size and constitution, and for the most part, are harmless to people unless they find a plentiful feeding ground."

"Feeding ground?"

"Yes, unfortunately, in our modern culture, we've neglected our spiritual health. When our spirit, with its stores of energy, becomes ill, so to speak, from the way we live, the choices we make. When we actually damage our spirit, it bleeds and is vulnerable to these creatures feeding on it."

"How horrible."

"Yes, and once they find a weakness, they seldom leave until it's repaired."

Of course, it did take her some time to figure out precisely what had happened at Pritchard Place that might have turned it into a conducive feeding ground. And then again, sometimes the causes proved quite obscure and sometimes not perceptible at all.

But the dreaming thing always left her uneasy and unsettled. One was always rather vulnerable in this in-between state. Things could be seen and known at this time that might be better off hidden. But as experience had taught her more than once, it was rarely her fate not to be in the know.

Of course, when it happened this time, she knew immediately where she was. But it didn't make it any more comfortable. She wasn't in her lovely double brass bed on Freret St. but, instead, was walking down a street late at night, or was it floating? She seemed to be moving rather fluidly, so it could well be floating. Mostly, it was dark, except for the occasional light emitted by the streetlamps every half block or so and, of course, the dim lights on houses. It wasn't her usual area of travel, but it had been earlier in the day, down Dante St.

"Now, what exactly did I miss?" Sending the question out, out to perhaps the universe, spirit guides, anything, or anyone who might be paying attention.

She frowned, realizing she was dressed in the dark purple silky pajamas she'd thrown on after a long relaxing tub bath earlier in the evening. Lucky for her, this was a dream. She certainly didn't want to be sporting her nightwear for public consumption. Elise paused again across the street from the old Warrick house and allowed her mind to expand.

Through the slotted fence, she could see the dogs asleep. They were the two that Martha Densford had described, but that she hadn't seen on her visit there. They were both asleep in the yard near the cobbled brick walkway leading up to the front door.

Again, she asked, "What should I be seeing?"

As she relaxed more deeply into this altered state, vision changed, and she allowed it, letting herself be perfectly peaceful. She could see the great house now, behind a sort of filter of color or rather colors as it was fracturing. There were yellow to golden hues and great splashes of blues being emitted from the ground floor. But beyond that, there was something else on the fringes, something closing in on the other colors. It was an ugly hue of red trying to seep inward, almost as though it was aggressively attacking.

Elise breathed deeply. What had she always said about the place? Oh yes, that was it, complicated. She could see that now. There were many layers at work here.

"Yes, isn't that always the way?"

And then, she was sitting up in her bed on Freret St, looking around. That voice had startled her right out of the dream. It was that strong deep male voice that sounded suspiciously like Joseph Mcginvale.

A Visitor on the Patio

6

"So, how about we go out for some breakfast Aunt Elise?" Caroline stared at her with her wide greenish eyes and a lovely smile plastered on her face. Beside her, on Elise's couch, Cassie sat with a similar expression, nodding. And standing near the front door was Jared, just looking a tad bit bored.

Elise glanced from one to another, wondering for not the first time that morning what exactly Cassie and her brood were up to. They had arrived on her doorstep just after nine, a bit early for them, Elise thought, for a Sunday morning. "Well, actually, I already ate. I had some toast."

"Toast, that's not enough. There's a wonderful breakfast place not far from here—at least you could get some coffee," Cassie enthusiastically pushed.

"What's going on?" Asking in a soft but steely tone.

"Told ya," Jared interjected flatly.

"Cut it out, Jared," Caroline snapped at him.

"Nothing Elise, we've just all been so busy lately. We haven't spent much time with you," Cassie said placidly, her smile having dimmed a notch.

"You saw me yesterday."

"I know, but it hasn't just been us, like old times."

"You know Cassie," Elise said, leaning in from the rocking chair on the side of the short sofa where Cassie and Caroline sat perched. "I'm not a charity case. I have a busy life."

"They're worried about you and this Mcgiver guy," Jared spat out with little animation.

"Mcgiver?"

"His name wasn't Macgiver," Caroline then turned to Elise saying sweetly. "What was it again, Aunt Elise?"

"Oh, you mean Joseph Mcginvale."

"Close enough," Jared commented.

"Now that's not really true, Elise," Cassie shifting uncomfortably after Elise gave her a hard stare. "Well, maybe a little bit. I don't know after you told me about him and that house—" she rambled on.

"The Warrick house?"

"Yes, Caroline and I just got an uncomfortable feeling. We think maybe you should steer clear of it."

"Oh, the house? Well, I doubt I'll have much to do with it or its owner. No real reason to."

◆

It was nearly eleven when Elise's front doorbell rang again. Just over half an hour ago, she'd said goodbye to Cassie and her bunch. They'd spent the morning together at a lovely little restaurant on the corner of Carrolton and St. Charles Avenues.

And there, she'd broken down and eaten her second breakfast with her sister and children. It was actually a delightful morning. And at present, she just intended to settle in on her back porch with a rather neglected book on growing exotic herbs when she was interrupted.

Her first thought was that perhaps Cassie had forgotten something, but then she hesitated at the door before she opened it. As was her custom, she checked the peephole, then took a step back. And she had been the one to claim she would have no further contact with Joseph Mcginvale. Well, it appeared she had spoken too soon.

Taking a deep breath and swinging open the door, he looked at her smiling broadly. "Well, Elise, I hope I'm not overstepping in returning your visit."

Frowning, though she consciously melded it quickly into a semi-smile. "I am surprised. How did you find—"

"Yes, I am a researcher, and it wasn't so very hard to track down an Elise Ashford living on Freret St. Am I catching you at a bad time?"

"No, no, I was thinking of having a cup of tea on my back porch."

"Would I be very presumptuous in asking to join you?"

"You, presumptuous, Mr. Mcginvale? I would imagine not," answering a tad bit wryly.

♦

The feeders, as she would call them, were sneaky. They hid from her as much as possible in the house at Pritchard Place. Some were relatively small, like the insects she'd seen on the walls, others the size of rodents, which were a bit peskier but still manageable. But then, there were the large ones, about human size, who came for a particular purpose, a weakness.

And, of course, they would come out at night when everyone was asleep. But when she would see them, she would notice a marked difference, particularly in her mother the next day. She would seem more irritable, more fatigued. And, of course, Elise began to put it together. The *things,* well, they were attacking.

She thought to confide this to Cassie, but honestly, her sister was so emotional that Elise didn't know if she could handle it. So instead, she watched and waited, quietly and all alone.

"You become vulnerable when you neglect your spiritual health."

"I'm not sure exactly what that means, spiritual health."

She remembered Dr. Rajun had smiled at her almost indulgently. They were sitting in her office at Loyola eating lunch together, as they had become accustomed to doing about once a week that summer. "In truth, it really doesn't have anything to do with going to church. All of us are comprised of the body, soul, and spirit — three important components, all very connected. The spirit has many lifetimes, many incarnations, but the soul is created for just this lifetime. And the body is the shell through which both live and essentially learn. But as I said, they are all connected."

"Yes, but what determines spiritual health?"

"Let me explain. The spirit makes itself somewhat vulnerable by incarnating on the earth. It needs to be protected and considered, or it can be damaged, wounded if you will."

"How do you wound it?"

"Oh yes in so many ways, ignoring the spiritual path chosen before birth, hurting others, hurting yourself, breaking sacred vows."

"What kind of vows?"

"All kinds, marriage, for instance, the marriage ceremony is a sacred one designed to protect the spirit. If those vows are broken, it can cause problems. You know, my dear. It isn't a judgment of right or wrong but rather a consequence of cause and effect. Any action, any choice, brings on a consequence."

And Elise had been silent, nodding, remembering the feeders at Pritchard Place and understanding that they just might have been a consequence of her parents' infidelity.

◆

"This is a lovely patio."

She was sitting on a black, wrought iron chair near a trellis of variegating roses that Cassie had helped her set up several years ago. Cassie had quite the gift with greenery that Elise tried to emulate but could never pick up the knack of. "Thank you," sipping her hot chamomile tea. Her stomach was still rumbling from the delicious omelet she'd eaten at La Madeleine's. This would teach her to remember to eat light in the morning and definitely not eat two breakfasts.

Elise calmly observed as Joseph Mcginvale methodically prowled the perimeters of her small garden. Sitting under the shade of an oak tree, she was content to silently watch him until he decided to tell her what he really wanted.

He paused at the back wooden fence just staring for a moment. In fact, he was staring at everything in her yard — her nice little stone fountain with its dragonfly effigies, the various prisms hung off the roof of the patio cover, her herb garden filled with lavender and sage. And then abruptly, turning on his heel, he sat down across from her at the small wrought iron bistro table, placing his tea on its uneven surface. "You seem to be a bit of an esoteric, Elise."

She hadn't expected this, well, this directness. "Why would you say that?"

Smiling, "Are we being candid?"

"If you wish to be Mr. Mcginvale."

"Your house, your ornaments, your manner, and dare I say your aura."

It felt dangerous, this territory that they were traveling into. "So, you must be a student of esoteric studies as well, Mr.—"

"Joseph, please."

"Joseph."

"Yes, although I haven't considered myself a student for some time."

Picking up her tea, Elise took another sip, considering. She didn't have Caroline's empathic gifts, which she, without question, could use just now. Though she did try to feel, feel where this was going. "Well in answer to your question, esoteric studies are an interest of mine."

He frowned unexpectedly, "And you have gifts in that realm?"

"Don't we all?" replying diplomatically. He then did something odd, began to strum his fingertips on the tabletop in a rather annoying manner. In fact, they were irritating the devil out of her. "Do you mind very much stopping that?" saying rather impulsively. "It is very annoying."

Looking a bit surprised and lifting an eyebrow, "Not at all," removing his hand. "Sorry, it's a nervous habit."

"And are you nervous, Mr.—hmm—Joseph?" she said a bit begrudgingly.

"No not nervous, more impatient."

"Really? Impatient?" Taking yet another sip of tea and having no idea how to respond to that.

"Would you like to know why?"

"I'm not at all sure, if I would."

"I, you see, I want something."

She took a moment to let that soak in. This was unexpected and confusing. She was not unacquainted with amorous suitors. But clearly, this man didn't seem to be making any kind of a pass at her — although undeniably, he was focused on her more intently than she was comfortable with. "Does this have something to do with your research Mr., hmm, Joseph?" It just felt so unnatural to call him that.

"Of course."

"And it involves—" Then she stopped, seeing a clear image of the old Warrick house rising in her mind.

"Yes, that's it."

Frowning explicitly, "What's it?"

"I could see it clearly in your mind."

Her eyes widened a bit in shock. "In my mind? What are you telling me, that you're reading my mind?"

"Yes, of course, Elise, ever since we met."

A Collector

7

It was something that she'd kept from Cassie. It had begun when she was about eight. Elise, as an impetuous youngster, had gotten in the habit of trying to answer the phone before anyone else could get to it. It was a Saturday, and her mother was shopping with her sister. So, she was bored. Quickly picking up the heavy receiver, because in those days, phones were cumbersome, it happened on this occasion that she was too late. Her father was already talking to someone.

"When will I see you?"

"For lunch, Monday."

"Not sooner? I miss you."

"We have to be careful. Ella may suspect."

"Are you sure, Thomas?"

"No, no, I'm not."

Elise had quietly put down the phone and vowed to herself to never try to answer it before anyone else again. She did mention it to Cassie once, but her being the little sister, she was brushed aside as having made it all up. So instead, she kept a silent vigil over the dark information that loomed over their happy home.

"Those things, creatures from other dimensions, seemed to affect my mother more than anyone."

"Yes, unfortunately, women are more susceptible. In some ways, they are more naturally spiritually sensitive by virtue of being able to give birth, but it also makes them more vulnerable. That is why they must be more vigilant in protecting their spiritual health."

"How could what my father did impact my mother that way?"

"It's the nature of unions, protected by ceremony or not. Once you enter into an intimate relationship, it impacts the spirit. You are connected by energy bonds. So, what your mate does can impact you, cause wounds of a sort."

"But what about people living together?"

"Bonds are still created by the nature of an intimate relationship, only there's no protection of ceremony if the relationship is problematic when people live together. Actually, it's more dangerous, in my opinion."

"Doesn't seem fair," she murmured.

"It's cause and effect. You must remove yourself from the mindset of judgment. Like touching a hot stove, once you know it burns, you might reconsider touching it again."

◆

Elise felt stunned staring at the placid expression of Joseph Mcginvale, acting as though he'd just told her something benign like he was in need of new tires. "Did you say you've been reading my mind?"

"I did, although it's not exactly reading, more picking up images, emotions, though I have to admit you're very well-contained, Elise."

"And I have to say you are abominably rude. How dare you violate my thoughts?"

There was a hint of a smile at the corners of his mouth at her last remark. She did not believe in violence, but she wouldn't have minded slapping that smirk right off his face just now. "Sorry you view it that way, Elise. It certainly wasn't my intention to upset you. But as soon as I moved into the neighborhood, I have to admit that I sensed someone of, shall we say, your particular gifts. And then, when you showed up on my doorstep."

"I was going for a walk," saying quite sharply.

"You felt the activity at the Warrick House and were drawn to it."

"I—" then pausing. She was letting her emotions get out of control, which wasn't her nature. "Activity?"

Another smile, glancing away and picking up her tea again and also wondering if she should ask him to leave. But then, if she did, she would never find out what all this was really about. Glancing up at him, his dark eyes were watching her intently.

"Stop it!" demanding abruptly.

He looked away for a moment. "Sorry, it's a habit."

And then, dark eyes were on her again. "Activity?" repeating.

"Oh yes, the house. You were drawn to what was happening there."

"You think so?"

"Explains your sudden interest. After all, the house has been sitting there on Dante St. a very long time."

"I have always felt something a bit off about the place."

41

"Of course."

"But that doesn't mean anything. I walked by because of the gossip. A new owner causes gossip in the area. It's natural."

"Undoubtedly."

"You doubt it?"

"That there's gossip? Not at all. There's always gossip. But you, being of such a heightened psychic nature, felt something else."

"And what do you think that is, Mr. Mcginvale?" replying pointedly.

Clearly frowning at her use of his surname. "This isn't how I wanted this to go."

She looked at him blankly, just raising one eyebrow quizzically. She'd watched herself do this. She actually did it quite well. "Well, best-laid plans."

"You've heard of the great esoteric figures in your studies Elise — H. Spencer Lewis, Annie Besant, Charles Leadbeater, Manly Hall, even Madame Blavatsky. All of them, as well as others, spent extensive time in New Orleans, studying here, finding something in this place of intense interest."

"It is a very old and historic city."

"A powerful city as well, energy points, frequencies."

"Agreed."

"Well, I am not only a researcher. I am a collector."

Slowly putting her tea on the table, now feeling something, something quite strong. "A collector of what exactly?"

"Rare esoteric materials."

"Is that why you're here?"

"Yes," he said slowly. "That is the only reason I am here. I am looking for something, something that has been hidden."

Breathing deeply, feeling a peculiar energy at his words, she could almost begin to see an aura now generating around him. It was of the palest blue color rippling with edges of gold. But it wasn't coming from him. It was connected to what he was saying. "You believe it's here."

"In the city, yes."

"The house, you think it's in the house."

"Yes, Elise, I knew our association would be helpful."

"I don't understand. If it's in your house, just get it."

"If only it were that simple."

"I don't—" Then, in her mind, the colors rippled in and out of vision, folding in on themselves.

"It was hidden, very carefully, precisely." His voice continued, but she was seeing well beyond him. "Not quite on this plane, but close."

"But you can't—"

"Yes, that's right. I can't get at it. That's where you come in."

Now focusing concretely on his face. His expression was stern, determined, and she wondered vaguely if this man might be dangerous in some respect. "Me?"

"I want you to help me find it."

"It? What exactly are you looking for?"

"Well, that's just the problem, isn't it? I'm not exactly sure."

◆

Her father's affair went on for some time. For years, she believed, although she couldn't be exactly certain. She was very young at the time, in her early teens, when she suspected it had ended. But then again, there was her mother. It was odd, an old high school friend she reconnected with briefly, perhaps a month, perhaps two. Of course, she had no direct evidence of involvement, just a feeling and her mother's absence from time to time when she and Cassie would get home from school. She supposed the situation with her father left her mother very lonely. But that didn't change the fact that this only compounded the problems in the house.

"So, the feeders were brought on by this?" she'd openly asked Dr. Rajun. There were very few people she could count on in her lifetime whom she could openly ask anything. Dr. Kavya Rajun had become one of them.

"No, not necessarily. I'm sure many people participate in such activity and come out of it relatively unscathed. These feeders, as you call them Elise, act very much like insects in our world. It starts with an infestation. No doubt, the house already had a less active infestation, and a new feeding supply stimulated their growth."

"So, how would you get rid of them?"

"Many methods, cleansing ceremonies, strong positive energy, but the most useful method would no doubt be starving them out, removing their food supply."

"We did move eventually."

"Hmm, impossible to say whether the next owners of the house had a similar problem."

Odd how interconnected a family could be. She didn't fully glean this at such a young age. But it seemed as though her father's actions, then later her mother, damaged them all in a way. Perhaps not an obvious way, but chipped away at their harmony, clearly their energy, the girls' self-esteem, and their mother's emotional well-being. Everyone and everything are so interconnected.

And the consequences, well, Elise kept them largely to herself. She would burn candles at night, in her room, in the hall. She'd convinced Cassie to do so as well because she did see the large one creeping into her sister's room one night. Sometimes, when she'd see them about, she'd tell Cassie that she'd had a bad dream and ask to sleep next to her in her bed. She didn't tell her why, but they kept away when they joined forces.

It was unnerving, living in a house with monsters when no one else knew. If it weren't for her stoic nature, she was sure it would have sent her quite off the deep end. But when she was fifteen, they moved from Pritchard Place, and in their next house, she didn't see the feeders again.

♦

"How can you not know what you're looking for?"

"I believe it's a book," frowning and looking quite bothered. "Or at least that's what I believe it was originally."

"Sounds rather vague."

"Things can be disguised, and energy can be—"

"Transformed," murmuring.

He looked at her a bit oddly. "Yes, you do understand, don't you, Elise?"

"No, I really don't understand this at all. And I believe there is quite a bit that you're not telling me."

Smiling now, "Well if you agree to at least come to the house this afternoon, I can attempt to answer some of your questions."

She thought to decline immediately. That would be prudent. But she didn't. She didn't say yes, but more than that, she didn't say no.

ALEXANDER WEIR

8

He walked with a heavy step off the porch of Elise Ashford's Freret St. address. He didn't know exactly what he'd expected, but clearly, what he got wasn't even close to what he had anticipated. The afternoon sun hit his skin a bit uncomfortably. He hadn't quite acclimated to the warm weather of being this far south. He wasn't sure he cared for it. But then again, that wasn't his concern when he began this process. He was on the hunt for something, something he'd traced here.

Something that frustratingly he couldn't quite get his hands on.

His feet took him down Freret St. on the way back to the house where he lived. But his mind was elsewhere, still on Elise Ashford's patio. She had sat there rather composed, listening to him talk about his quest for a mystical object as though they were discussing nothing more important than the weather.

He found her a difficult, complex woman. Someone he'd actually sensed strongly in the area before they'd even met. And it had taken some time before he recognized that he would need her help. In fact, it wasn't until last night when he felt her astral self outside the house, that he knew she would be able to see things that he, for some reason, could not. She had specific gifts. And if only—

And then he stopped, stopped, and looked around. He'd gone too far, too preoccupied. He'd completely missed the corner turning onto Dante St. The question became now how to get Elise to do what he wanted. And he laughed to himself. Yes, he was sure, not having known her for very long, that trying to get Elise Ashford to do something she didn't want to do was an absolute impossibility.

♦

"Elise, are you all right?" Cassie asked with genuine concern from the other end of Elise's cell phone. Good question. He'd left over an hour ago, and she was still as unsettled as she had when he'd walked out of her front door.

"I am just feeling bothered."

"Do you want to come over?"

"No, no, I can't," shaking her head, even though no one else was in the room. "I have things, so many things to take care of."

"Oh, all right, are you sure?"

"I—" another question. Was she really sure of anything now? She sank into the rocker, in fact, the very same white rocker she'd had her mother buy for Mrs. Lavender. Why she hadn't gotten rid of it after all these years was anybody's guess. "I was wondering, Cassie, if you ever think about it — if you ever think of when we lived at Pritchard Place."

There was silence on the other end of the line for a few moments, and Elise realized now that they seldom talked about their childhood there. "Sometimes, I think a lot went on there that I do try not to think about."

"Yeah, Mom, she was very sad."

"Yes, she was very unhappy a lot of the time."

"Yes, I remember. It's just, I don't know, difficult to let go of all that sometimes."

"You know you should, Elise. You do deserve to be happy. It wasn't really fair, you being so young and, well, seeming to know so much. I—"

"I have to go, Cassie," saying quickly. "I'll talk to you later." And then she hung up. All of this was hitting her so oddly, churning things up. The tears were coming down her cheeks, but she didn't want them to. She didn't want to feel the deluge of emotion from the past that seemed to be threatening her.

♦

He felt her approaching the house at nearly four. It surprised him. He'd pretty much given up on her today, so he checked out the front window and indeed saw Elise Ashford crossing the street to his house. He had no idea what had made her decide to help him. He had sensed a deep restlessness within her. Perhaps that was it. He didn't really care. He would take advantage of anything she was willing to offer.

♦

She walked into the empty den of the old Warrick House. Yes, that was right. He'd said something about the furniture coming next week. Houses did indeed have a personality, and moving across the polished wooden floor of this one, she understood that this was a house of secrets.

"I had pretty much given up on you."

"There are things I need to know," walking slowly around the perimeter of the large room.

"Of course," he said quietly, seeming content to stand by the staircase and watch her.

And then she stopped her circling and turned to face him. "You."

Frowning, "Me?"

"Ever since we met, I've almost choked on your name. No, well, that's not exactly what I meant. I mean Joseph Mcginvale. There's something uneven about it."

"Uneven?"

"Yes, names, they sort of mesh to people and yours—"

"It doesn't mesh?"

"Are you making fun of me?" They did have an odd sort of rapport that she wasn't sure yet if she enjoyed.

He sunk down onto one of the bottom steps of the staircase. That was the thing about having no furniture. It forced a lot of standing. "I wouldn't dream of it. Well, all right, I admit it wasn't the greatest idea. In fact, it wasn't my idea but rather my editor's."

"Your editor?"

"Yes, it's sort of a secondary pen name that I was going to develop for some works of fiction. So, I decided to use it once I bought this place. Sort of keep a low profile, gossip, and all, as you did so adroitly point out."

"So, your name isn't Joseph Mcginvale?"

"No, Elise, my real name is Alexander Weir."

She simply stood there, staring at him, more than a bit stunned. "I have several of your books. But the pictures on the book jackets—"

"A model, nice looking old chap. I like to travel about inconspicuously."

Slowly, absorbing this curious information, "I see, so why is a famous metaphysical writer so interested in this place?"

"As I explained earlier, there is something important here, something important enough to be very well hidden. Hidden, I believe, somewhere around the turn of the century."

"Is this place really that old?"

"No, but there was always something here, a park once, part of a plantation before it, and other dwellings, one occupied once by the great Madame Blavatsky."

"Madame Blavatsky? And you believe she is the one that left something there. I mean, in that house that was here."

"Something very old and very alchemical."

"But how could it still be here, Jo—oh damn, I haven't a clue what to call you now."

"Alex."

"Really, Alex?"

"Or Alexander."

Grimacing, "Fine, we can try that. But quite honestly, I have no idea what I have to do with this."

"I don't believe in coincidences, Elise."

"Well, that's very nice for you, but what exactly does that have to do with me?"

He smiled, seeming to enjoy sparring with her. "I believe you can help with this. I believe you are meant to."

Taking a deep breath, "Is there more you can tell me?"

He nodded, "Yes, of course, but you'll have to come upstairs into the study."

This was uncomfortable, not liking the feeling of being rushed through an unclear series of events. "Well, at least I hope there are chairs there."

He did seem oddly gratified. "Oh yes, and more than one."

♦

As they ascended the curving staircase at the Warrick house, Elise's mind was flying. Alexander Weir, how could that be true? She had books by Weir sitting on her bookshelf spanning from medieval occultism to Rosicrucian philosophy to an examination of Satanic ritual through the centuries. And this was what gave her pause. What was he really after, if indeed he could possibly be who he claimed? And the thing he sought, what could possibly really be hidden in such a manner, and what was its nature—good or evil?

She followed him down a narrow hallway on the second floor and into a door he opened. The room itself was rather large but the ceiling low, giving almost a claustrophobic air. Immediately noting several boxes, a few folding metal chairs, a desk with a laptop, various stacks of binders, books, this was all.

"Where are you sleeping?" she asked with distraction.

"Down the hall, in one of the bedrooms," he answered slowly.

"There really isn't any furniture. You weren't planning on staying here at all?" Murmuring.

He turned to her, "No, not really, not once I found what I was looking for."

Walking around the room and feeling the strange fluxes of energy, "You thought it would be easy."

He frowned. She'd noted he did that often as of late. "I've had some experience with these matters."

"Objects hidden in a different dimension?"

"Mystical items, ceremonies, ancient rituals."

"I thought you said this was turn of the century, hardly qualifies as ancient."

He pulled up a nearby folding chair, sitting. "No, that's when it was hidden, but its actual age? Well, that's unknown, as well as the age of the techniques used to put the item in safekeeping. They very well could have been ancient, or old at the very least."

She continued to scan the room for anything that might be helpful. "All of it still sounds a bit vague. Who did you say did this? Madame Blavatsky?"

"There is mention of this in her writings of New Orleans of the codes of Tempus."

"Tempus, isn't that a reference to time? And she claims to have seen these codes?"

Eying her with curiosity, "So many questions Elise. Yes, Tempus is a reference to time, and no, she did not claim to have seen these codes directly."

"Then how—"

"Her references to the matter are almost encoded secretly within her writing. It took trying many, many types of ciphers before I could crack the limited information I did."

She looked to him speculatively, "So, you've been at this awhile?"

He shrugged, "On and off, but yes, for decades, and even that only gave me scant information."

"But enough to guide you here."

Nodding slowly, "Yes, enough for that. And to know that whatever Madame Blavatsky hid was very unique."

"But you really have no idea what you're dealing with."

"Isn't that the thrill of discovery? To bring to light what is unknown."

Answering a bit somberly, "I suppose, but sometimes things are hidden for a reason."

His dark eyes narrowed a bit. "There is always risk when the achievement is great. But all of that aside, Elise, I predominantly wanted to see if you could feel anything here."

"Oh, I see. Pick my brain, then send me on my way."

"I rather imagined you wouldn't want to be too involved, or could I be wrong, Elise?" he asked quietly.

She stared at Alexander Weir, wondering, indeed, how involved she wanted to be. "What do you want exactly?"

"Well, first I'd just like you to wander the place and see if you can pick up on anything."

◆

"You know, you need to develop layers, layers of protection. Your gifts run so deep, Elise, but you do have to function in the world."

"Which world?" she asked without humor.

"Yes, good question," Dr. Rajun had answered. "I suppose the one where you have your feet firmly planted."

And the question was still floating around there somewhere in her mind. Which world, indeed?

Elise took a deep breath. She did not reach out, just simply allowed that veil of energy she so meticulously placed around herself every morning to slowly drop. She did not close her eyes because what she saw was already changing, the room fluctuating as its own unseen energies became apparent to her naked eye.

She breathed more deeply, allowing herself to relax into this new level of reality. It now became fully apparent why this room felt so claustrophobic. It was full. Full with things hanging off the ceiling, writhing in and out of the walls, scurrying across the floors — creatures varied, low ones like the feeders at Pritchard Place but more of them and more varied in size and appearance. The sight and recognition of what she was seeing actually flipped her stomach violently into nausea.

"You must have difficulty sleeping in this house," murmuring aloud. She assumed Alexander was still in the room somewhere, but she couldn't see him. She was so absorbed in this other level of reality. One so close its inhabitants crossed back and forth with ease.

"Yes, I've picked up disturbing energies here."

"That's one way to put it," answering with a tad of sarcasm. They were scurrying closer to her, particularly the smaller ones that thought they could connect quickly and then dart away. But she concentrated on emanating stronger energy to repel them.

It was not only clear that the place was infested but that they'd found an ample supply of energy. "This thing, whatever it is. Would it give off strong energy?"

"Yes, it's old, mystical."

"Varying types of energy?"

"Yes."

She nodded, "It's bleeding, bleeding this energy."

"How do you know?" he asked.

But she didn't answer. She closed within herself to return. But found, unfortunately, too late that she'd expended too much as the darkness reached for her.

THE CALVARY

9

"Why don't they go away?"

"It doesn't have anything to do with you."

It was the fever. This was what everyone was telling her. It was all hallucinations from the fever she was having.

"The medicine the doctor gave will help soon, Ellie." She'd forgotten the nickname her mother had given her, but she seldom used it — just at times like this one, when she was particularly worried about her. Her throat was painfully sore, and she was hot, so hot, so achy and uncomfortable.

But even that wasn't the worst part. It was the things she saw all over the room. The feeders had come in, and they weren't afraid the way they usually were. They smelled the energy she was losing. Their appetite overcame their wariness. "They're everywhere," murmuring, nausea rising in her stomach.

"They're not real," her mother whispered soothingly, dabbing her forehead with a cool cloth.

And then her eyes met Cassie's. She was hovering in the doorway, watching her intently. And she knew at that moment that Cassie believed her, believed her completely.

Elise's eyes fluttered open. The light stung, but then her vision began to adjust. She was lying on something, something very stiff and uncomfortable.

"You've been sleeping on this?" asking vaguely.

"It's a cot."

"It's horrible."

"You get used to it." He was bending over her, staring down at her in a way that made her feel terribly awkward. "Are you all right? You passed out."

Sitting up and feeling a further swirl of dizziness. "Yes."

He was frowning again. He seemed to be frowning at her more frequently as if she were some perplexing puzzle piece. "What did you see?"

"I don't think this will work," she said flatly. "We're outgunned here."

"Outgunned? You mean there are impediments?"

"Alexander, this code you're after. Is it alive?"

"Alive? What would make you say something like that?"

"Energy, it seems imbued with much active energy."

"Did you see it, Elise?"

Hesitating, "No, but I saw a lot of things that are clearly feeding off of it."

♦

"I don't understand," Cassie was staring at her with her wide blue eyes. The same compassionate blue eyes she remembered staring at her from the doorway of her bedroom so long ago.

It was a gamble. Elise had considered walking out the front door of the old Warrick house and leaving Alexander Weir to his own devices. She wasn't at all sure his motives in wanting to obtain this mystical code were completely selfless. Perhaps it would be better to leave it be. But there was that something nagging at Elise.

She'd sensed the swarm of feeders in the house, but there was something beyond that. She sensed pain as though something was unnatural there, causing the bleeding of energy. Like on Pritchard Place, spiritual wounds attract the parasites.

So, she'd made a choice. She called Cassie and asked her to assemble her kids and Max, of course. Elise had great confidence in his skills as a psychic. She asked that they meet her in an hour on Prytania St at Cassie's house. And as succinctly as she could, with Alexander Weir at her side, she attempted to explain the situation.

"Mr. Weir, we are all at a bit of a loss here as we don't really understand what you are asking us to look for," Max stated rather stoically.

"Please call me Alex," he replied, looking around as though he were a bit overwhelmed. "The reason that Elise and I are being so ambiguous is that we are not entirely sure what the nature of the object is."

"What are you saying? That it's not the same now?" Jared asked from across the den.

"According to the writings of Madame Blavatsky that I could decipher, it was some sort of artifact that she obtained during her travels to India.

"What does that mean originally?" Caroline questioned quickly on the heels of Alexander's answer. He looked from one person to another with a calm but intense expression. Elise had the feeling he was just beginning to appreciate how formidable they could be.

"We suspect that whatever this was might have transformed in some manner. I sensed quite a bit of energy connected with it and also things feeding off that energy," Elise tried to explain.

Cassie looked a bit confused, but then again, Elise had never completely shared her experiences at Pritchard Place with her. "You're talking about parasites," Max said sternly.

"Parasites?" Caroline echoed, looking at him oddly as though perhaps he'd kept some personal secret from her.

Nodding, "Things that feed off astral energy."

Again, Caroline was looking at him, confounded. "Things? What kind of things?"

"Mostly unseen," he murmured. "Unless—"

"Unless, of course, you can see them, which I do," Elise said matter-of-factly. She could feel Cassie's eyes on her. No doubt she was remembering now things that had been said and unsaid.

"Elise," Cassie directed to her somewhat abruptly, rising from where she'd been sitting in a nearby rocking chair. "I'd like to have a private word with you upstairs in my bedroom. Caroline, why don't you get some iced tea for everyone else. We won't be long."

◆

It changed things. Once you began to see what most people didn't. It changed things, and it also changed you. Elise remembered the house on Pritchard Place fondly in the early days with its great big granite steps leading up to the large porch in front of the house. There were days she would sit on the hard-stone floor of that porch staring out into the street below watching the people as they passed by and sometimes not. Sometimes allowing herself to drift elsewhere, to hear the murmurings and whispers of the past around her so close that it would only take a gentle tear to breach the veil that held two worlds apart.

It wasn't an unpleasant feeling, but it always did tend to make her separate, different from those around her.

♦

"What's this all about?" Cassie asked moments after she'd closed her bedroom door behind them.

"We need your help."

"We? You barely know this man, and yet you're willing to put all of us at risk to help him find this unknown thing. Do you really know his motives? Just because he writes about esoterics doesn't make him altruistic. He wants to sell his books for profit."

Elise quietly sat on a rose-colored chaise lounge chair that Cassie had positioned near her bed. "I don't remember making money or being successful as being a crime. Max sells books. I imagine he's sold some of Alexander's books at his bookstore."

"Do you have a crush on this man?"

"You know not everyone is in this world thrashing about looking for their great love."

Cassie's eyes narrowed. "Then what are you looking for, Elise?"

"I," she hesitated. Damn, her sister's unvarnished honesty. It was definitely unsettling at times. "I'm looking to help, looking to do something that will help."

"And you think helping Alexander Weir get his hands on this mystical thing will be of help?"

"I didn't say I was doing this for him. Something is in trouble in that house. Whether or not we hand it over to Mr. Weir remains to be seen."

Cassie opened her mouth to speak, then hesitated, as though the impact of what Elise had said finally hit her. "So, you are saying you are not beyond double-crossing Mr. Weir."

"He is not my focus in this."

Cassie had put her hands on her hips and then let out a bit of a sigh, which told Elise quite decidedly that she now might be willing to get on board with her plan. "So, you're using him?"

"He's using me to get at what he wants, and I'm using him to help, well, whatever this thing is now."

Cassie shook her head. "I just don't understand how it could have changed into something living. How is that possible?"

"So many things are possible, Cassie, so very many things."

Cassie eyed her a bit shrewdly with her sky-blue eyes. "All right, Elise. I trust you, and I am trusting you with the well-being of my family."

Nodding slowly, Elise felt the weight of that last statement in a profoundly tangible way.

MADAME BLAVATSKY

10

Max Gravier had followed Caroline Breslin into the kitchen to fetch the iced tea that no one in the den seemed particularly enthusiastic about receiving. The whole situation struck him as unsettling. He'd known Caroline's Aunt Elise for nearly a year now, and she'd never seemed to him to be a particularly rash person. She appeared thoughtful, measured in her actions, wry, and even caustic at times. But for her to dive headfirst into something so potentially fraught with uncertainty, seemed bizarre. As he remembered, she'd been very alarmed some months back hearing about their strange paranormal encounters at the Hotel Mandolin. She'd even called them all reckless.

Caroline pulled the glass pitcher out of the refrigerator in complete silence and was now taking glasses out of the cabinet. "What is it?" he asked.

Focusing on him with a grim expression. "I don't like it."

"What? This plan of your aunt's?"

"Can we call it that? Does it qualify as a plan?"

"Um, how about a vague idea."

"And this guy, this Alexander Weir, you've heard of him?"

"He is a very prolific writer. I sell quite a few of his books at the bookstore."

"What do you think of him?" she said, squinting her eyes as though trying to focus on something over his shoulder in the direction of the den.

"I don't know. There hasn't been much time to—"

"I don't like him," she spat out suddenly.

"Really? Why? Are you picking up something from him?"

Looking at him intensely as though she were trying to concentrate, then shaking her head. "I don't know. It's just a strange feeling that he's hiding something."

Max nodded. That was fair. Something about this whole thing definitely didn't add up. "So, you want to sit this one out?"

Shrugging, "I don't see how we can. Aunt Elise is set on it. I can tell, and there's no way Mom will let her try to do this on her own."

♦

"So, what exactly do you want us to do, Aunt Elise?" Jared asked pointedly. Alexander glanced at her, then back to Jared. He seemed content for the moment to relinquish the reigns of control, clearly given that he had little choice if he wanted their help.

"I'd like us to meet at Alexander's house tonight. We're going to need a lot of energy to get past the feeders to the heart of what is going on there."

"You're suggesting that we help you travel to wherever this object resides now?"

"Not just Elise, of course," Alexander interjected. "I'm going as well." Staring at him for a moment, then nodding, she willfully concentrated on blocking her thoughts from him, as she had advised Cassie to do. She dared not let him know what she was up to.

◆

Cassie insisted that she feed the group who had gathered at her house with take-out pizza from one of Jared's favorite restaurants on Magazine St. The dinner had been pleasant, jovial, with Alexander mixing in comfortably with stories of his travels. But Elise felt a frisson in the air, a fracture of sorts, and occasionally she caught Max's eyes on Alexander. Not exactly with suspicion, more as though he were studying him. Max had his doubts, of that she was certain, but that was all right. Elise had hers as well.

Then dinner had ended, and they all packed up in their various cars to head to Dante St. and the old Warrick mansion. Cassie had insisted Elise ride with her, leaving Alexander Weir as the odd man out, traveling in his car back to his house.

"I called Peter, but he is tied up tonight on a case," whispering to Elise, sitting next to her sister in the passenger seat.

"Why are you whispering, Mom?" Jared asked from behind them. Caroline and Max were following them closely in Max's Jeep.

"I don't know. I just feel rattled. I thought it would help to have Peter along."

"You need to calm down, Cassie," Elise answered in normal tones. "I just basically need you all to be there."

"So, you and this Alexander Weir can fly off astrally to God knows where. I don't really understand this, Elise. It isn't at all like you."

Taking a deep breath, that was true enough. This wasn't like her at all. But she still felt compelled for a reason that even she couldn't identify, like closing a door that had been left ajar. "Make sure you guard your thoughts. He reads minds."

"Aunt Elise, I don't know about this guy."

"Just be cautious, Jared, you too, Cassie. Be very cautious."

♦

"This isn't like you."

She heard the words repeated from somewhere, moments before, decades before.

As they all crossed the threshold of the old Warrick house, it certainly should have felt full. But, as soon as the heels of her shoes echoed across its naked wooden floors, all she could feel was emptiness.

"Why don't you leave him?" she'd asked her mother blatantly. It was so long ago, on moving day out, out of the house on Pritchard Place. And its wooden floors were naked as well, naked and gleaming, as they'd been cleaned, waxed, and buffed, made ready for the new occupants. God help whoever they were because the house was still full of them, full of the feeders just looking for a new food supply.

"This isn't like you, Elise. This isn't like you to say something like this to me."

She was fifteen, just on the edge of everything. But still, it was that peculiar age when some considered you an adult but many still a child. And, of course, some didn't consider you at all. "I know you're not happy. This could be a new beginning to start over."

And she remembered her mother looking at her as though she were speaking nonsense. But she didn't have to be an empath to understand. Some people were simply comfortable in their unhappiness. It was familiar, safe in that respect. The fear of change of what was unknown was more daunting than existing in their present state of misery. It was a subject that Elise didn't bring up again. There was no point. Some things didn't change.

"Elise," Cassie whispered beside her. And she drew herself back to the present.

"Take a look around everyone," she said, adding directly to Alexander Weir. "If that's all right with you." He nodded, which she took as an affirmation. "I'd like everyone's impressions before we try anything else."

Cassie looked at her somberly and then walked across the den, Jared trailing without enthusiasm behind her.

Max and Caroline hadn't moved. They were just standing holding hands in the center of the spacious room. Elise noted that Max took a deep breath, then turned his attention to Alexander. "Mind if we nose around upstairs?" saying flatly.

Alexander seemed a bit surprised but then gestured to the staircase with his hand. "By all means."

Without hesitation, Max headed in that direction with Caroline wordlessly following behind him. Alexander was looking at Elise quizzically. "Should we go with them?"

Shaking her head, "No, best not," meandering over to a large window and moving the drapes aside to look into the front yard. "Are the dogs put up?"

"Yes, I have a gated area in the back. Are you sure this is a good idea, Elise?"

"I guess we'll find out," she answered softly.

♦

"I feel dizzy," Caroline whispered.

"I know," Max answered as they slowly walked down the skinny hallway upstairs in the Warrick house. Her hand was clasped in his, helping to stabilize all the rampant emotions she was feeling. People, people everywhere, upset, anguish, pain, all of it was coming over her like a flood.

"Be careful," Max murmuring beside her. "Put up some sort of barrier to protect yourself."

"But it doesn't make sense what I'm feeling. It's too much for it just to be the people who've lived in this house. It's like a deluge of emotion."

"I know." She could detect great strain in his voice. "Clearly, there is something here that doesn't meet the eye. But it's unstable." Max stopped for a moment, pausing in front of a closed door, and staring at it oddly.

"Max—" she began, but he squeezed her hand, silencing her."

"There is something here," he murmured aloud though almost to himself. "Something important just on the other side."

♦

"What are we doing?" Jared asked.

He and Cassie were standing outside, just staring into that small, drained pool on the brick patio of the house. "We're supposed to be feeling."

"I feel that is a waste of a good pool," he grumbled. Cassie continued to pace slowly back and forth across the small New Orleans-style courtyard space. Her skin was irritated, her head throbbing uncomfortably with a stabbing pain in the center of her forehead — the third eye, as the esoterics called it. "So, what is wrong with the place, some sort of haunting, leftover negative residue?"

"I don't know. It feels more active than that—" she started to say, then stopped, stopped, because a woman was standing there now, standing near the door of the house dressed in white robes. It was an older woman, not terribly tall. Her hair graying but long, pulled up in a bun. "Jared," quickly motioning to the figure. "Can you see?"

He was quiet, gazing solemnly in the same direction. "Yeah, the lady over there."

Cassie thought to move toward her but was rooted to the spot. It was her eyes staring at her, large dark eyes, old, intense, but filled with sadness. Clearing her mind to receive any impression, there were none except powerful waves of profound regret.

"What does she want, Mom?" Jared asked slowly.

"I don't know. But it's clear she's very upset about something."

♦

"Maybe we should go up there."

"Give them a little more time," Elise said. He was agitated. This she felt clearly. Alexander Weir didn't like not being in control, but she wanted to give them all the time they needed before—

"Before what, Elise?" saying a little too coolly. Damn, he'd caught her. She'd forgotten about his gift.

Frowning, now looking at her almost speculatively. "Not my only gift," he said calmly. "I was hoping you'd be willing to help me with no tricks. But there are other ways."

And suddenly, he was beside her, roughly grabbing her arm. "Now close your eyes, Elise, because we're going to do some traveling."

67

An abrupt dizziness and then a swirl of color before she felt herself hit the cold wooden floor of Pritchard Place.

Pritchard Place

11

"Max, are you sure?"

He heard Caroline's voice, but something was pulling him, something so strong that he didn't feel capable of fighting it. So, with little choice, pushing open the door, he walked inside.

Max simply stood there for a moment on the threshold looking around. It was impossible where he found himself. But then again, his mind was muddled, confused. Maybe he was supposed to be here, maybe.

And then she walked into the room, looking at him with a wide smile. "We could go work on the bookshop today if you like." Smoothly taking him by the hand, gently pulling him further into the den at their Calhoun St. address, her warm arms encircled him — the arms of Chloe, the wife he'd buried four years earlier.

Caroline's head was spinning. Max had opened the door upstairs, walked inside, and then shut it behind him. She'd reached out, turning the knob frantically, but it was locked now.

"Max, Max," she yelled in a panic. But there was no answer, and the door wouldn't budge. She grabbed the sides of her head with her hands. A blinding pain in her temples had hit her as soon as he'd left. What in the world was happening?

◆

"Mom, what are you doing?"

"She wants us to follow her," Cassie answered quickly. The figure in the long robes had disappeared into the house, and Cassie hurried behind her.

"Are you sure—" but then she couldn't hear Jared's words anymore. A loud buzzing in her ears was drowning out everything else. The woman moved, or should she say floated, through the house's rooms until they were in the large den again. But now it was empty. Elise and Alexander had vanished.

Startlingly, she felt Jared behind her grabbing her arm, "Mom." The loud noise in her ears was gone. It was just Cassie and him now. The woman also had vanished. "She's gone," murmuring, feeling as though she was in complete confusion.

Almost in response to her desperation, Caroline barreled down the stairs, her eyes wide with fear. "Mom, Jared," she nearly exploded, forcefully grabbing Cassie's arm that Jared was also hanging onto. "Something's happened, something not good."

"I know," Cassie saying slowly, feeling the chill that now permeated the house on her skin.

◆

Elise ached everywhere. Slowly sitting up, she struggled against a powerful fog of confusion that had settled across her brain. The only thing that was clear was that she was now on the floor of her childhood home at Pritchard Place. She could even smell the lemony floor polish that her mother used to apply to its well-worn, wooden floors.

With painful disorientation, continuing to look around — the sofa, the television, bookcases, the small decorative touches her mother had always placed around the house were present, even fresh-cut flowers sitting in a vase on the table near the entrance. But what was made crystal clear by the pains shooting throughout her forty-five-year-old limbs was that she was not a teenager anymore.

And then there was a creak on the heavy wooden staircase across the room. The old woman stopped on the bottom stair staring at Elise with a curious expression. "Well, dear," Mrs. Lavender spoke to her in a voice that she never remembered having heard in exactly that way before. "It seems that you are on my side of things now."

◆

"Chloe," Max whispered with disbelief as he continued to receive hugs from the wife that he was quite certain was no longer in the land of the living.

"I know we just bought the building, but I'm itching to start renovating. Aren't you?"

Looking around once again, just to convince himself of where he was, his eyes widened. He remembered this place, their place, where they would have stayed if Chloe — if she hadn't become ill. "I think I need to sit down," murmuring in total bewilderment.

His wife's beaming and radiantly healthy-looking face pulled back from the hug to look at him with a concerned expression. "Are you feeling all right, Max?"

He stepped back, sitting down on the pale blue loveseat positioned against the wall. It was crazy. He remembered when they'd picked it out together. "I don't know. I've got a bit of a headache now," he rambled, trying to wrap his head somehow around what was happening.

Chloe frowned a bit, seeming a tad disappointed. "Well, how about I get you a cup of tea and some aspirin, and then we can talk about our plans?" Managing a slight smile from realms unknown, then nodding. His wife, the one he was quite sure he'd been bereft of for some time, bent over, giving him a soft kiss. "I love you," she said, before she left him sitting there quietly in disbelief.

Max leaned back on the loveseat and closed his eyes, attempting to clear his mind. Everything was muddled. That much was clear, painfully confused. He must get hold. It was the only way he could deal with anything. Methodically, he tried to retrace his steps. What was he doing just before he found himself here?

The recollections were shrouded and now almost felt like imaginings he'd made up.

There was a girl, that other girl with the green eyes. And she wanted something, something he was having trouble remembering. Trying again to clear his mind of all the confusing debris. What was she saying to him, calling him in that house, that old house? And then there had been a door.

The more he tried, the more his head exploded with the headache. Something, something didn't want him to sort things out.

"*Max*," she whispered, "*Max*," again, more urgently.

And then he found the name on his lips. "Caroline," he murmured, slowly opening his eyes.

Chloe was standing there in front of him with a steaming cup in her hand. "Who is Caroline?" she said with little expression.

"Max went into a room upstairs, and I can't get to him now. It's locked, and he won't answer me." Caroline explained rapidly in a panicked and breathless voice.

"Did you see Aunt Elise up there or that Weir guy?" Jared asked.

Caroline looked at both of them with mounting horror in her eyes. "No, they're gone too?"

Grabbing her hand and then Jared's quickly and firmly. "Now calm down, both of you, calm down. We have to have clear minds to deal with this."

Caroline's eyes were filled with fear, but her mother could see she was trying to steady herself. "Okay, what do we do?"

Canvassing the room, the large empty room. "The three of us need to stick together. No one wanders off on their own now, agreed?"

"Mom, do you think this guy pulled something? I don't think Aunt Elise really trusted him." Jared said intently.

Caroline's eyes widened as she pulled away from Cassie's grasp. "She didn't trust him. Then why did she do this?"

Cassie looked at her, trying desperately to find the words for something she didn't really understand. "It was something she felt she had to do."

◆

Elise somehow found the strength to come to her feet, although she was trembling all over. She stared across the room at Mrs. Lavender, though she had no idea if that was truly her name.

"Flora," the old woman said in her rather rough, crackly voice. She stepped off the bottom step and moved towards Elise, sort of shuffling.

"I thought you'd left this place."

The old woman looked at her oddly, then around with confusion. "Have you died?" she asked Elise a bit blankly. It was a question that Elise now felt obliged to consider with some gravity.

"I don't remember that." And she realized that her mind felt quite uneven and fractured now. "No, I don't remember that."

Mrs. Lavender, or rather Flora, nodded slowly as though considering what she'd said. "Then how are you here?"

Elise looked around again with displeasure and then saw something scurrying, scurrying quickly up the wall. "I'm not sure, Flora. But I suspect someone put me here." Again, she saw movement, this time across the floor then under the couch.

"They're afraid of you now," Flora said softly. "But they won't be for long."

◆

"Someone I used to know."

Chloe sat down beside him, smiling, then handing him the tea, but something else was in her eyes. He'd forgotten how possessive she was at times. "Not someone I should worry about?" teasing softly.

He breathed in deeply, painfully. He tried again to remember those things that something did not want him to. "I don't think you should worry about anything. But I do need to get rid of this headache," taking the aspirin from her other hand.

"Well, maybe you need to lie down for a bit."

He nodded, feeling acutely uncomfortable with a woman he'd spent so many years married to. "Maybe so."

She stood up, simultaneously looking concerned and a bit frustrated. He remembered now how she used to walk the tightrope between such conflicting emotions. "Okay, well, I have some developing to do in the dark room. That should give you an hour or so to feel better." Again, she leaned over and gave him a quick kiss. And then, as she left the room, she said laughingly, "And no more talk of this, Caroline. You don't want to make me jealous."

Max watched her leave with a feeling of mounting pressure and confusion. He put the tea down on a nearby glass coffee table and leaned back again, closing his eyes. He must sort this out, sort this out quickly, because for some indefinable reason he felt a clock was ticking somewhere.

FULL CIRCLE

12

The three members of the Breslin family stood in the den of the old Warrick house, holding hands and closing their eyes in concentration. "Just try to clear your minds and feel. See if you can feel where the others are," Cassie instructed. She was working hard to quell the panic within her. All it would do was muddle her mind more than it already was. Caroline would focus on Max, so she would try to track Elise. Breathing deeply, she pictured Elise in her mind, surrounded by white light. She then allowed herself to be guided to where she was. But as she did, as she attempted to follow the very delicate but insistent thread that would lead her to Elise, she felt an impediment, something tangible blocking her.

"I can see Max," Caroline whispered shakily. "But he's caught somewhere, somewhere confusing."

"I've got Aunt Elise," Jared interjected. "She's talking to some old woman in a house somewhere."

Cassie opened her eyes with confusion. "I can't get anything. Something or someone is getting in my way."

Jared opened his eyes as well, staring at his mom with a grave expression that made her forget how young he was. "Maybe you're supposed to stay here."

Caroline, looking at her intently now, added, "Why don't you let Jared and I try to help. And you anchor us."

"Send you two off as well to who knows where?" And then a movement across the room caught her attention. The mysterious gray-haired woman dressed in long robes now stood serenely watching them. It should have been unnerving seeing her there, but for some reason, her presence reassured Cassie. And then the woman suddenly nodded as though to confirm their plan. Cassie looked back at her kids. She didn't like this, but she was desperate, as though she was stumbling around in the dark. "All right, let's attempt a meditation."

Jared looked down at the floor. "Okay, but I wish this guy had a few pillows, at least. What is he, a Spartan?"

"What is he? Good question," Cassie echoed slowly as she sank onto the floor to achieve some sort of comfortable seating position. "Now you guys know the drill. But if things get too dicey, concentrate on coming back immediately. You understand?"

Caroline nodded in agreement, "Yeah, of course."

♦

Elise was cold, not cold from the outside but from the inside. It was as though her just being in this state of existence was somehow barren.

"It's always chilly," Flora commented beside her.

"Are you reading my mind?" Asking as she continued to methodically roam around the den of her old Pritchard Place address.

"No, I thought I heard you say something. It's easy to mistake the two here."

Elise grimaced with irritation. Clearly, she was somehow now in that ghostly dimension — spirits trapped in the in-between, not having moved on, clinging to life for some reason. But the question remained, why was she here? Had she been sent here for some purpose? "The people who live in the house, do you ever see them?"

"Oh, you mean the other ones, mostly not, just once in a while, but it's no use trying to talk to them. They're deaf to everything that's real."

Looking at the old woman a little sadly, unfortunately, it was clear what was real and what was not was all a matter of which side of the veil you were sitting on. Again, her mind rushed over with some kind of fog. There was so much confusion here, muddled thinking as Dr. Rajun had called it. And there was something she was supposed to do but couldn't quite—

And then she jumped in surprise at a sound at the front door, some sort of soft knock, "Did you hear that?" asking Flora, who had settled into a green lazy-boy chair in front of the TV.

"Hear what, dear?" answering with distraction, staring at some static on the television. Apparently, something unseen to Elise had gotten her attention.

So instead, Elise headed to the front door, where the light tapping continued. "Who's there?" directing loudly through the heavy wooden door. And she waited, not really knowing what she expected. But after several moments, there was an answer.

"It's me, Aunt Elise, Jared."

A hesitation, muddled thinking again. Jared? Cassie's Jared, but he was just a little thing. No, wait a minute. That was a while back. "Go away," Flora said. Elise didn't realize that she'd gotten up to stand beside her.

"Aunt Elise, are you there?" the voice from the other side said a bit more emphatically.

"We don't want your kind here," Flora hissed in response.

"Stop that!" Elise scolded, trying to nudge the old woman aside, who was now deliberately blocking her ability to open the door. Cold, when she touched her, permeable cold went through her. "Jared, I'm here!"

He was jangling the knob from the other side. "Unlock the door Aunt Elise," but the old woman continued to try to block her.

"We don't want none of your kind here," Flora repeated harshly. "Go away, you demon!"

"That's my nephew," Elise spat out, then, with exasperation, gave Flora one great push that sent her tumbling onto the floor. Sighing with exhaustion from battling with the old crone, she unlatched the deadbolt and tugged the heavy door open to find Jared standing on the threshold with a bit of a scowl on his face. "Who's in there with you?" an undeniable edge in his voice.

"A very confused old woman," answering as he walked into the house. "It's all right, Flora," she said, offering her a hand to help her to her feet. "This is my nephew."

Flora glared at them both. "There's not enough room for so many here."

Elise turned to Jared, who was looking at Flora with a pronounced look of dislike. "What are you doing here?"

"Mom sent me to bring you home."

"Home?" she repeated. The fog was clearing a bit, just a bit, with Jared's presence. He must have brought some energy with him.

"We had no idea what happened to you."

And then it flashed across her mind with clarity. Alexander Weir had done this, had sent her here to Pritchard Place for some purpose.

◆

Max leaned back on the sofa. It would be easy to simply collapse into this space. It was familiar, being here with Chloe, the life they had built. It had taken him time, so much time to put it behind him and allow for new things to grow, to allow for her—

In his mind now, he could almost see her, although it was foggy, insubstantial. But it was getting closer, the image melding into something more concrete, tangible. "Caroline," he whispered aloud.

And then her hand was on his. Slowly opening his eyes, she was standing over him. "Max!" she said joyfully.

Standing up and shakily grabbing her shoulders with his hands. "Caroline, what happened?"

"Max, don't you remember the room in—"

"The Warrick house." It was coming back in a painful rush. He remembered the room now, stepping into the room with all the light, and then he was here, here—impossible!

"Caroline, are you all right?" he said in real concern.

And then abruptly, a voice from across the room sliced through everything. "Max! Who is this?" He turned now slowly to Chloe, who was looking at them with a tinge of accusation in her eyes.

◆

Elise headed wordlessly upstairs in the house at Pritchard Place. Jared was behind her, following with rapid footsteps, calling, but she paid no mind. There was something here, something that she needed to see. She stopped in front of the door of her old bedroom. It was closed, and she hesitated, hesitated going inside. Just behind her, Jared stopped as well. "What are you doing, Aunt Elise? We have to find a way back home." He said a bit breathlessly.

"I know," answering more calmly than she felt. And then she pushed open the door. The room was only dimly lit by a single lamp covered with a pink lampshade. But the young girl sitting on the floor with the long dark hair looked up at her with wide green eyes. "Now I remember," Elise said almost to herself.

"Who is that, Aunt Elise?" Jared asked with confusion.

"Why it's me, of course."

ELISE

13

Caroline stared at the woman across the room with mostly surprise and a bit of shock. She had long blond hair and was actually very lovely. Walking a bit closer and repeating what she'd said to them only moments before, "Max, who is this woman?"

Max, still holding Caroline's arms, let his hands slowly drop. "This isn't going to work," he said slowly.

The blond woman looked at him with confusion. "What are you talking about, Max?"

"You're not Chloe," he said with a very quiet but deliberate tone.

Caroline's eyes widened at the revelation as she stood there feeling a bit like she'd been punched. "Chloe, your wife, Chloe? But she's—"

"Been dead for quite some time," he finished rather coldly.

The blond woman sighed a bit, shaking her head. "You must not be feeling well, Max. You're talking nonsense."

"Am I?" he responded. "You had me fooled for a little while, but this illusion you've concocted isn't going to work, Mr. Weir, if that is really who you are. I won't help you find what you're looking for."

The softness in the blond woman's face suddenly dissipated, replaced by a very stern expression. "Well, no matter," she said with steel in her voice. "I just needed you out of the way long enough for the others to find it."

And in a swirl, Max was no longer in his former house on Calhoun St. but rather in the den of the old Warrick House with an unconscious Caroline in his arms.

◆

"It's all right," Elise said slowly to her younger self.

"Are you a ghost?" the girl responded rather matter-of-factly, which reminded Elise, well, of herself.

"No, no, I'm not, but I am lost."

The younger Elise was dressed in a set of dark purple flannel-type pajamas with yellow daisies on them, which Elise actually did clearly remember having. She crossed her legs and peered at them intently as though trying to see them clearly. Oddly enough, Elise did remember this encounter rather dimly, recalling it as a dream long ago. "I don't think I can help you." The girl said to her.

Elise frowned, sitting on the edge of her childhood white metal daybed. "That's too bad."

"Is that really you?" Jared asked from the doorway. Elise had nearly forgotten he was there with her.

"Me, at about eleven."

"Twelve," the young Elise said briskly.

"You were a cute little thing," Jared remarked. "But still prickly, why are you sitting on the floor?" he asked.

"She's waiting for them."

"For what?" Jared said.

"Monsters," young Elise said curtly. "They usually come out at night."

"Monsters!" Jared repeated emphatically. "Did she say she was waiting for monsters?"

"They're not really monsters Jared," Elise said. "I like to call them feeders."

"Oh, feeders, well, that sounds much better. Don't you think we should be getting out of here, Aunt Elise?"

Young Elise smiled a bit mischievously. "The boy is scared."

"Hey, you, I'm not scared."

"Settle down, Jared, it's all right. Don't you see we're here for a reason? There's something here, close."

"We're here because your nutty friend sent you here, some-how—" he rambled on, looking around the room dubiously, then to a window whose curtains were not drawn. "Wait a minute. It's not nighttime. It was the middle of the day when I knocked on your door."

"Time is different where we are, Jared."

"What does that mean? Where we are?"

"This place in between."

Young Elise was looking at them again, rather solemnly. "Are you sure you aren't ghosts?" she said with little emotion.

"Well, reasonably sure," Elise answered with a bit of trepidation in her voice.

"Oh God," Cassie rasped. Moments before, she had been sitting in a circle with Jared and Caroline in a meditation. And now, after a strange swirl of dizziness and shift in her vision, Max was beside them with Caroline slumped over in his arms. Next to her was Jared, silent, sitting with his shoulders hunched and eyes closed, still firmly holding her hand.

Max glanced around quickly, clearly trying to soak in what was going on. "Don't break the contact with Jared." He said emphatically and then started patting Caroline's face, clearly trying to get her to regain consciousness.

"What happened? Is she all right?" Cassie asked frantically. But he wasn't listening. He was focusing entirely on Caroline.

"Come on, Cara, come on," he muttered with anxiety in his voice. He was on his knees, holding her securely in his arms, but something was wrong. "We were together, but it shouldn't take her this long for her astral self to return to her body." He closed his eyes, clearly focusing and Cassie was certain, trying to find Caroline. Breathing deeply, Max then slowly opened his eyes, staring across the fractured circle at Cassie. Haltingly, he spoke, "Somehow, on the trip back, something happened. She was diverted by something or, rather, someone."

"Where is Caroline?" Cassie said with mounting panic.

"I don't understand what's happening, but it's clear she's with Elise now."

◆

Elise wasn't sure when it had occurred, but the door to the younger Elise's bedroom was now closed. "Did you do that, Jared?" she asked. He was now sitting beside her on her childhood bed. But there wasn't time to answer because, almost as she spoke, a very soft knock started on the other side of the door.

Jared's eyes widened. "Who could that be?"

"It might be my sister, Cassie," the young Elise said. She was still sitting on the floor and had pulled her knees up to her chest with her hands wrapped around them.

"Really?" Jared said.

Elise frowned as the tapping continued, becoming more insistent. "I don't know. It feels odd."

Jared stood up, looking a bit more alarmed. "What if it's one of those monster things, feeders, whatever you call them?"

"They don't usually knock," young Elise commented dryly. "They sort of slither."

"Well, that's wonderful!"

"Calm down, Jared," Elise said firmly. No need for hysterics here, particularly in such an environment so ripe for hysterics. "Maybe it's Mrs. Lavender. Mrs. Lavender is that you?" she called out loudly to the door.

And what she thought she heard in response was a muffled, "No, it's not."

Jared looked at her with wide eyes. "It's not Mrs. Lavender."

Elise stood up from the bed and walked over silently to the closed door. She took a deep breath, clasping the now very cold, golden doorknob in her hand, and turned it. "Be careful," young Elise murmured.

And then she pulled the door open. On the other side, Caroline stared at her with disheveled hair and wide, frightened eyes. "Oh God, Aunt Elise."

"Caroline, how in the world did you get here?"

She shook her head slowly, looking nearly panicked. "I don't know. I was with Max, and then we were separated, and I found myself downstairs with all these things."

Jared nearly yanked his sister into the room, quickly closing the bedroom door behind them. "Things? What kind of things are you talking about?"

"Horrible slithery, and insect-like, all different kinds, and they kept buzzing, looking like they were going to eat me alive," she rambled on disconnectedly as she sunk onto the bed.

"Those are the monsters," young Elise said, still looking reasonably placid.

"Feeders," Elise corrected. Everyone was alarmed enough without embracing this idea of monsters. "But why so many? I don't remember there being so many."

"It's gotten worse," young Elise said, eying her older counterpart shrewdly.

"Hmm," Elise murmured as she considered things. This wasn't exactly the past she remembered, although granted, her recollection could be somewhat flawed. "Caroline, you said you were with Max."

Caroline looked a ghastly pale color. Whatever had happened to her had clearly taken its toll. She nodded, "Yeah, Max had gone into one of the rooms upstairs. And I couldn't get to him."

"At the Warrick house?" Elise offered. It was odd. Just having Jared and Caroline here had largely restored her memory, which had been so foggy when she first arrived.

"Yes, so Mom, and Jared and I attempted a meditation to facilitate—"

"An astral journey," Elise filled in.

Caroline nodded again slowly, seeming more than a bit unraveled. "Jared went looking for you, and I went looking for Max. And found him." Then she stopped, her face looking very pensive at the memory.

"Where did you find him, Caroline?"

She looked up at Elise with a trace of a pained expression on her young face. "He was at his old house with," then she hesitated, "with his dead wife."

"His what?" Jared nearly exploded.

"That's right, with Chloe."

Elise wrinkled her nose a bit as she remembered her mother doing, "That's very odd," she said slowly.

"Ya think?" Jared chirped in.

And Caroline was just sitting on the edge of the bed looking at them close to tears. "Then, after I got there, Max told her he knew she wasn't Chloe. And then we got separated."

Elise took a deep breath, attempting to let all of this information sink in, but before she could speak, young Elise conveyed her very thoughts. "Sounds like some sort of an illusion. Is that what this is? An illusion?"

The Closet

14

Cassie stared at both of her children, Caroline lying in Max's embrace unconscious and Jared still in his meditative sitting position but slumped, eyes closed. A fiercely cold wave of fear wrapped around her heart. Everything had somehow gone totally out of control. "She's with Elise? Where? How could that be?"

He was sitting on the floor near them, holding Caroline's unconscious body. "That's what I can feel. She and Jared are with Elise but somewhere else, in another house," he opened his eyes, staring at her directly. "Feels like another time."

"What? Another time? What does that mean?"

The panic was rising uncontrollably in her, and then suddenly across the room, near the staircase, she could see that woman again — the older woman in the white robes. "Please, please help us," Cassie rasped desperately. Max turned, looking in the direction of where she was focusing her pleas. But he was silent, just staring at the staircase. "Max, can you see her?" But he didn't answer, just continued to peer in that direction. "Max!" she nearly yelled.

"Yes," he said calmly, his attention returning to Cassie. "I can see her."

She waited, completely bewildered by his odd change of mood. "What's wrong?"

"I need to go help them," he said with little emotion. "They're all in trouble."

"What!" Cassie exclaimed, ready to jump out of her skin.

His eyes focused on her, very intense, very solemn. "Cassie, please listen to me. I know you're scared, scared for your children, but I need you to stay calm. It's important that I go and try to find them. But I need you to stay here, to anchor us all and stay strong. Can you do that?"

There was something in his voice, an odd resolve that made her trust his words. "All right, Max."

He nodded, closing his eyes. "I'm going to try to follow their path now. Just be calm," he whispered. And then there was silence, and as she glanced across the room, she saw that even the woman in the white robes had disappeared.

♦

"Do you hear that?" Jared asked.

Elise looked around with a bit of trepidation. It was something that she heard now and had heard long ago — like a scratching inside the walls.

Caroline looked around, her green eyes so wide in her pale face. "What is it?"

"Them," the young Elise said, pulling her knees closer to her slight body with her arms.

Jared was standing in the center of the room, seeming quite spooked. "What, are we just supposed to wait for them to pounce on us?"

"They don't usually do that," the young Elise said quietly. "They usually like to wait until you're asleep." And then she glanced around the room a bit suspiciously. "But this feels different."

"It is different," Elise said standing up. "This doesn't exactly feel like the past."

"Maybe it's some kind of illusion, like Max and I were in."

Elise shook her head, sensing, sensing a thousand conflicting impressions. "I don't think it's exactly that either. Alexander Weir, or whoever he is, wanted Max out of the way, so he created that illusion with his deceased wife. But he definitely wanted me here to find something."

"That artifact thing?" Jared asked.

"If that's really what it is," Elise said slowly.

Her eyes focused now on that younger version of herself sitting quietly but attentively on the floor. "Elise," she said directly to her. "Where do they come from, mostly?"

"Which ones?" she asked.

"The big ones."

The young girl pursed her lips a bit as though in concentration. "The big ones I've seen come out of the closet."

Jared's already wide eyes widened a bit more. "The closet! What about under the bed?"

Elise looked at him a bit critically. "Calm down, Jared. These things, feeders, do have a nest."

"Aunt Elise, you really think their nest is your closet?" Caroline said with confusion.

"No, no, of course not, but it might be connected to somewhere else."

"Aunt Elise," Jared began with a much more strident voice than Elise recalled hearing from him before. "First off, that closet," he pointed to it emphatically, "cannot be connected to anything else, and second why would we want to search for their nest?"

"Jared, you forget, my dear, we are on a different plane of reality. Things don't connect in the same way here, not like the natural floor plans of a house. We are dealing with flows and channels for energy. That creates unique connections and passages. And yes, we need to discover the source of things. The nest would indeed be at the very heart of this matter."

Caroline stood up from sitting on the bed, "Okay, Aunt Elise, what do you want to do?"

Elise glanced across the room. "I want to go inside the closet."

Jared shrugged, looking a bit as though he would reluctantly fall in line. "Okay, okay, little girl," he said to young Elise, "looks like we're all going in your closet."

In a quick motion, she was on her feet, a look of excitement flashing across her youthful features. "Well, I'm going too."

Elise smiled at her and nodded. Yes, she remembered that age. There was no way she would have been left behind. She walked across the room to the closed door. She remembered it well. It was a large walk-in closet crammed, with old toys and games as well as her clothes and some of Cassie's winter wardrobe. But there always seemed to have been a draft within, whose source she couldn't identify. "Everyone, stay close behind me," Elise directed, as she cautiously opened its entrance.

Taking a deep breath, all there was ahead of her was blackness, but she hit the light switch just inside the door to no avail. "Bulbs burned out," young Elise informed her from somewhere behind.

"Okay," she said, taking a first step inward. It was so much larger than she remembered, large enough for her to walk forward several yards and fit the line of people behind her quite comfortably inside.

"What now?" Jared asked. "I can't see a thing, just darkness."

"Can you see anything, Aunt Elise?" Caroline asked. But Elise didn't answer, just found herself continuing to walk forward. There was something ahead, a dim light beyond, and then she nearly ran into a partially open door.

"I don't remember my closet being this big," young Elise said.

"It wasn't back then," murmuring. She pushed that mysterious door further open and found herself walking into a bit of an unstable cramped room, incredibly humid, with unpainted wooden beams cutting across the ceiling. Glancing around the stacks of boxes, plastic totes, and a few old bicycles, it dawned on Elise where they were.

"It's the attic," the younger version of herself declared.

"So, your closet connects to the attic?" Jared offered.

"You can't apply the normal rules of physical life to this place," Elise commented, but her eyes now focused on a movement in the shadowy part of the unevenly cluttered room.

"Oh God, is it one of those things?" Caroline said shakily.

And then the figure moved out of the shadows. Max stood in front of them with a grim expression on his face. "I've been waiting for you to get here," he said quietly.

THE ATTIC

15

Elise felt a swirl around her as though everything had shifted. The very ground where her feet were planted didn't seem all that firm. But then the momentary fracture in her vision cleared, and she was still in the humid attic of her childhood home.

Caroline had walked over to Max while Jared had settled himself on a stack of cardboard boxes, looking dismal. "I think we all need to leave here as soon as possible," Max said.

"I can't leave. I live here," the young Elise said rather petulantly.

"Aunt Elise, I think Max is right. The reason we were sent here couldn't be good. And there are those things all over the house."

"Too many of them," Elise murmured.

"Too many of what?" Max asked with gravity in his voice.

"The feeders, they seemed to be swarming. It was not like that when I lived here."

"She's right," the young Elise commented dully. She was now sitting on top of one of the old bicycles parked in the attic, a purple one. Elise did remember having a penchant for purple back then. "There's a lot of them now."

"Why, why so many now?" Elise said aloud but mostly to herself. She was pacing across the attic, well, as much as she could in the small space it afforded her.

"And where are they?" Caroline said softly. "I thought there was some kind of a nest here."

"There are so many people here," young Elise threw in.

"Yes, that's right. Our energy is probably repelling them now."

"Wait a minute," Jared interjected. "I thought you said these things feed on energy."

"A certain kind of energy, yes, the kind that comes from spiritual wounds. Our spirits bleed or lose energy when they are injured. Much like a physical wound bleeds."

"Elise," Max said slowly, "all of this doesn't change things. We need to get back. There is a danger for us here."

She focused on Max Gravier, frowning a bit. He liked to take charge, and although this seemed to endear him to Caroline at times, it definitely rubbed her the wrong way. "Yes, there is danger, but there is also something here, something that needs our help."

"Something that Alexander Weir wanted you to find for him?" Max replied.

She pursed her lips. "Yes, all of you go back. I'm staying until I figure this out."

"For Pete's sake Aunt Elise, we still don't know what we're looking for," Jared said with irritation.

"What did he say? It was an artifact or a code?" Caroline asked.

"Can we trust anything he said?" Max stated rather forcefully. "Who do you think put us in this predicament and the last one?"

"That's right," Elise was finding it hard to breathe within the cramped space. It was so stuffy. "He wanted you out of the way. That's why he sent you off to that illusion while—"

"While he sent you here," Max said slowly. "This could be an illusion as well."

Young Elise hopped off the bike, landing on her feet very lithely. "That's what I said."

Elise crossed her arms in front of her, that odd feeling of complete disorientation covering her again. "So, you think this is an illusion?" turning to Max.

"Perhaps," he replied.

She frowned again, couldn't help it. "So, what would the point be if he was really after this—thing?"

There seemed to be a moment, a hesitation. And then he shook his head, smiling a bit oddly, smiling in a way that began to make her skin crawl. "You're very good, Elise."

She took a sharp breath. "So, what do you call yourself? Some sort of sorcerer, illusionist?" she directed to Max.

Caroline had stepped away from him, looking at him suspiciously. "What's going on?"

"I prefer the word thaumaturge, although it is archaic."

"Thaumaturge? A bringer of miracles?" Elise emphasized with a tinge of disgust. "You do think highly of yourself."

"Aunt Elise?" Caroline said shakily.

"This isn't Max," Elise said flatly.

And then quickly, so quickly that she didn't have a moment to react, there was a sudden surge of energy and an almost electric crackle through the air. Elise had squinted her eyes shut to protect them from the sparks she thought she saw, and then she slowly reopened them. She was still in the attic, but Caroline, Jared, and the young Elise had vanished, and Alexander Weir was now standing where Max had been. "I appreciate this, Elise. Without all of you, I would have never found its hiding place."

Elise glanced around, now feeling them circling, rasping noises, antenna thrashing about. They wanted to pounce. They wanted to feed. "You aren't even Alexander Weir, are you?" she said with contempt.

"I am many things, but most of all, I am the man who will control the *tempus edax rerum*—time itself, the devourer of all things."

THE THAUMATURGE

16

Caroline lurched in Max's arms. The return had been fast, too fast. She gasped for air as she opened her eyes, staring into the blatant concern in his blue-gray ones. "Max," her voice cracked with exhaustion. Then he pulled her into a sitting position and into a strong hug.

Beside them, Jared opened his eyes as well but started coughing abruptly, as though he was struggling for air. "Jared," Cassie said with franticness, patting his back.

"Stop beating me, Mom," he managed to get out.

"What happened?" Caroline asked weakly.

"You were sent back for some reason," Max said gravely.

"More like shoved back," Jared nearly croaked, standing up and then looking around the room in confusion. "Where's Aunt Elise?"

"She didn't come back," Max said, helping Caroline, who was still trembling, to her feet.

Cassie's blue eyes were wide with alarm as the gravity of what he'd said soaked in.

"Max, I thought you were going to bring them all back."

The expression on his face was stonily grim. "I never got there."

♦

Everything was in a swirl, confusion. It was clear that she was losing energy. She could feel it slowly draining from her, and creepily she suspected the source was the things hissing and slithering around the attic. Undeniably, they now seemed very emboldened that she was the last soldier standing.

"What is all of this? An illusion on your part?"

The thaumaturge, because she dare not call him Alexander Weir — decidedly that man's name had been tarnished enough — was standing in front of her looking quite self-satisfied. The truth was now she had no idea who or what he really was. If nothing else was clear, it was that this man had quite a self-inflated opinion of himself. Bringer of miracles indeed!

"Don't be so critical, Elise. Remember, I can read your mind, and the weaker you get, the easier it is. Oh yes, you asked if this is an illusion. Partially I suppose, though I'm not exactly sure because I didn't choose it. It did."

"What does that mean? It did?" Her mind was clouding over, and she struggled against it. But it was getting hard to talk, hard to think.

"The entity that I've been looking for, it's been hiding for some time and evidently found refuge with you, with your memories."

She looked around blankly. All she could see was the attic, boxes, old stuff, and a few of her grandmother's hats strewn here and there. She could remember her and Cassie playing with them so long ago. "You're not making any sense."

He frowned exaggeratedly, and she wondered why exactly he had to act like such a bastard. "Now think, Elise. Let's finish this. It has been hiding somewhere in your attic, but where?" he droned on, moving closer to her. She felt a violent repulsion toward the man now. He must have worked very hard before to disguise his true nature. Again, he frowned, and she wished she had the energy to smack that ugly smirk right off his face. "Why bother thinking Elise? You might as well speak your thoughts aloud. It seems to me as though you're doing so anyway."

"You must just love the sound of your own voice," she spat out with venom.

He shrugged a bit and still seemed as though he was enjoying all of this so much. "It's weak, you see, being drained by those parasites for so many years. The ritual that was used to conceal it was flawed. It couldn't sustain. It couldn't help but be injured by it over time. I have to admit that it's taken a good while to bring its defenses down to a manageable level. But I have been working at it for so very long."

She felt a stabbing pain in her heart from so much energy loss. "You brought the feeders to the Warrick house," she said slowly.

"Well, there were some there already. There always are. We, humans, are messy creatures, stupidly making ourselves vulnerable to all sorts of attacks. But I have to say I did encourage their growth. It was a tedious way to get at what I wanted, but that old woman who'd placed it there for protection did an admirable job, albeit not a perfect one."

"Old woman?" Elise asked.

"Yes, she was considered one of the masters. Thought it best to hide and protect something potentially so powerful."

Elise suddenly saw a vision in her mind — a face. It was a face that she'd seen in many books over the years, Madame Blavatsky.

And for the first time, in what seemed like an endless interlude, she felt a rush of hope.

◆

Cassie found it difficult to breathe. She was caught somewhere between rage and panic—more than anything, she hated to feel helpless. "Now, we can't just give up! We have to find Elise."

Caroline, who was leaning against Max, looked at her with wide helpless eyes. "Mom, I feel so weak, so drained."

Cassie steadied herself. She had to be the calm one. Both of her kids were looking at her like they'd just returned from the frontlines of the battlefront. "Now, where were you all when you last saw her?"

"That house you two grew up in," Jared said.

"The house at Pritchard Place?"

He shrugged, "I guess. We had traveled from Aunt Elise's bedroom closet to the attic."

"The attic?" Max said a bit incredulously.

"Aunt Elise said things connected differently there because we were in a different plane of reality," Caroline explained weakly.

"Who else was there?" Cassie quizzed, feeling as though there was something they might use here.

"Aunt Elise, Jared, me, and you, Max," she said slowly.

He looked at her blankly. "But I wasn't there, Cara. I tried to reach you all but hit a brick wall."

"I know," she said softly. "It wasn't you. It was that Alexander Weir in disguise."

"Oh yeah, and you forgot that kid," Jared said.

"What kid?" Cassie asked.

"Well, evidently, it was Aunt Elise when she was little. She said she was twelve."

"Elise?" Cassie murmured.

"It must have been some sort of illusion," Max said. "Like what Weir pulled with me."

"But what was the point?" Cassie asked.

Max shook his head, "It's clear he was looking for something. Whatever he thought was hidden in this house."

"So, why bring Aunt Elise to her old—" Caroline's voice trailed off.

"Attic," Cassie finished her thought as her eyes drifted to the ceiling. "They must have one here somewhere."

Jared looked up, speculating, "How would that connect to Pritchard Place?"

"I don't know," Max said. "But let's give it a try," he barely finished because the Breslin clan was already headed for the stairs.

♦

Elise stepped back, further away from the creature. It flashed across her mind, the word creature, although he looked the same as he had the first time they met. That was back when he was using the name Joseph Mcginvale and then Alexander Weir, and now, well, whoever, or dare she say whatever, the hell he was now.

"Labels, Elise, labels," he murmured, slowly encroaching on where she was retreating across the attic. "You're too weak now to block me, and I'm certain you'll lead me to it now. It's inevitable."

What had he called it? She couldn't—

"Tempus edax rerum, but I prefer to refer to it as the time bender."

She sunk onto a plastic tote near the staircase that led downstairs. If she could only get back to her room, she could close the door and— she shook her head. Her mind was becoming so muddled. "What does that mean, time bender?"

He laughed, and it wasn't even a good evil laugh. Whoever he was, he sucked at this. "How did you think you ended up here in your past?"

"This isn't my past," she felt as though her throat were closing up with the extreme fatigue.

"Well, I'm sure it's not the one you remember, but there are always levels. What did you call them — planes of reality? Perhaps, this is just one of those."

"Can you just manage to answer a question straight? Or are you entirely incapable of doing that?"

He looked displeased. Evidently, she was taking some of the wind out of his sails. "The answer is that I wasn't responsible for bringing you here. I just followed. It did."

"It, what is IT? Is it alive?"

"Hmm," he said in a sickeningly indulgent manner. Again, she wholeheartedly wished she had the energy to give him a good punch in the gut. "Life, what constitutes life? Perhaps a question for the philosophers to debate." But then he moved quickly to her side grabbing her arm with one of his hands and squeezing painfully. "So, Elise, it's time to help me find now what I am looking for." It was worse than just the pain of his grip. His hand felt like fire, burning through her cotton shirt straight into her flesh, scorching her. "Illusions, I must tell you, can be as painful as reality. So, tell me now? Where is it hiding?"

Then across the attic, Elise heard rustling and saw movement from the shadows. At first, she assumed it was one of the feeders, but then she knew it wasn't. The figure stepped out of the darkness looking at them both with a stony expression on her face. It was her younger self. The one that Elise had thought disappeared with everyone else. "It's all right," she said, speaking directly to the creature. "I'm not hiding at all."

The Time Bender

17

Jared was the first one to reach the landing on the second floor. He looked for any entrance on the ceiling, but there was none. Following Cassie and Caroline, Max rushed quickly just behind them. "These old places usually had a doorway that opened onto a staircase leading to the attic," he said.

"But which way?" Jared was looking down a rather long hallway filled with doors.

"Maybe we should split up," Caroline said.

But Cassie's stern voice cut in on the discussion. "No, we don't separate again. We take them one at a time," pointing to the first door at the end of the hall.

"Okay," Max said. "But let's hurry," he couldn't shake the feeling of urgency as he turned the first doorknob.

◆

She remembered those, wearing those pajamas, the purple ones with large yellow daisies on them—something her mother had bought for her. "You need to hide," she whispered to her younger self.

The girl looked at her with wide green eyes filled with compassion and then turned sternly to the thing squeezing Elise's arm. "I'm not hiding. Let her go."

The man who'd called himself Alexander Weir looked down at the little girl with some confusion. "Can't be," he murmured.

But then the young girl reached up with her hand dragging her flat palm along his chest until Elise saw a red oozing sort of glow seeping out of him. "You should hide now," young Elise said. "They're so hungry, and you're bleeding."

His eyes were wide in shock as he stumbled back, clutching his hand to his heart area. "Can't be. You're too weak. Can't be," he kept saying almost to himself.

And then Elise saw them come out, out from everywhere, slithering, crawling, the winged ones flying, but they were swarming all over him. The girl held out her hand for Elise and said quietly. "We have to get out of here."

And as she touched her, Elise could feel the pain, all the energy she'd lost, and something else — an endless stretch of vision forward and backward. But then the young girl slumped against Elise and suddenly collapsed. So, instinctively, she scooped her up in her arms.

♦

They walked through the attic at the old Warrick house. Caroline was amazed at how tremendous it was, stretching across the length of almost the whole ground floor of the structure.

"What are we looking for?" Jared asked.

"Some connection," Max said.

"Like the closet," Caroline murmured, reaching out with her feelings for her Aunt Elise. "I don't understand. I feel close to her," she murmured.

"So do I," Cassie echoed, wandering around the expansive room. It felt so tangible like her sister was next to her. And she couldn't understand why she couldn't see her.

And then suddenly, across the attic, Cassie saw the woman in the white robes standing there quietly, looking at all of them. "Mom, do you see—"

"Yes," Cassie said, and then the woman turned to look across the great room where a door opened that Cassie didn't remember seeing before. Right in front of them, Elise stumbled into the room, and she was holding someone in her arms. Cassie's eyes widened. She couldn't believe what she was seeing. She recognized the young girl, so still in Elise's arms. She recognized her sister from so long ago. "Oh God," she said, walking up to them.

"Aunt Elise, are you all right?" Caroline said.

But Elise was silent. She was focused entirely now on the woman holding out her hands for the girl. "Will you take care of her?" she asked.

And then the woman smiled, gathering young Elise in her arms. Just as she did, the child stirred, looking at Elise and the rest of the people in the room. "Thank you for letting me have your strength, so I could find a way to leave," she spoke in a soft voice to them all.

Elise felt tears running down her face, and she wasn't entirely sure as to why. "I don't really understand what's happened."

The dark-haired child smiled at her, and it stirred memories. "I can make this easier for all of you," she said quietly.

Elise smiled, "But he isn't gone, is he?"

"It doesn't matter," the child answered. "Just close your eyes." Elise looked around at her family, "Everyone," her younger self murmured. And they held hands and then did as she asked, closing their eyes. For Elise, that was the last memory before everything changed, and she heard the rumble of thunder over her head.

♦

Elise looked upward, hearing the sound of thunder emanating from the darkened clouds. She glanced back across the white patio table to Martha Densford. "I'm sorry, Martha. What did you say about the old Warrick House?"

"Oh, just that it's still on the market. They can't seem to find a buyer for the old place."

Elise nodded, sipping her tea. And she remembered now the very intricate dream she'd had about that very house just the night before.

Finis

More Books by Evelyn Klebert

A Murder in the Village
And Other Mystical Tales of the Ouachita Mountains
6x9 Softcover & Hardcover 274 pages
ISBN 978-1-61342-459-9
ISBN (Hardcover) 979-8-27615-496-1

At the foothills of the Ouachita Mountains, into their ancient heart, and even perhaps into nearby unexplored dimensions, slip into a series of supernatural short stories.

A clash of shapeshifters on sacred grounds, a compromised witch desperately fleeing a witch hunter, and a ghost in search of his murderer are only a few of the tales that dot this paranormal landscape.

Take a mystical diversion that could very well land you in a realm, at the least unexpected and at the most horrifying. But what is clear is that no one, ever, will emerge as they were before.

The Alchemist's Bride
6 x 9 Softcover & Hardcover 230 pages
ISBN 978-1-61342-454-4
ISBN (Hardcover) 978-1-61342-455-1

From a young age, Emmeline Lescale has been raised as an outsider by her aunt's family on the lavish estate of Belle Coeur in Vacherie, Louisiana. Ostensibly an orphan, she is treated as an unpaid servant. But in her twenty-fifth year, with her eyes on a dismal future, something radically changes.

Her father, a renowned physician who has ignored her existence most of her life, suddenly insists that she come to live with him. And New Orleans in the 1880s seems like no place for a proper young lady, especially when her father is embroiled with a mysterious young doctor whose interests venture deeply and dangerously into the world of the supernatural.

Jack Fallon, the protege of Emmeline's father, lives a life filled with secrets. His home, deep in the French Quarter on Bienville Street, is much more than meets the eye. And before too long, he draws Emma into the crosshairs of an existence that questions the nature of reality itself.

The Broken Vow
Vol. 1 of The Clandestine Exploits of a Werewolf
6 x 9 Softcover & Hardcover 204 pages
ISBN 978-1-61342-133-8
ISBN (Hardcover) 978-1-61342-420-9

In the heart of every man, there is a history. In the heart of every monster, there is a story. In this first installment of The Clandestine Exploits of a Werewolf, Ethan Garraint is on a vendetta that begins in the heart of the Pyrenees with the fall of Montségur and leads him to the streets of New Orleans nearly five hundred years later. But the person he chases isn't really a man anymore, and Ethan has been a werewolf for almost a millennium. With the aid of a gifted seer, he is on a blood hunt that will culminate in a journey that crosses the line between heaven and earth and ends somewhere in between.

The Story of Enid
Vol. 2 of The Clandestine Exploits of a Werewolf
6 x 9 Softcover & Hardcover 254 pages
ISBN 978-1-61342-453-7
ISBN (Hardcover) 978-1-61342-456-8

What happens when your one true love reincarnates, and you just happen to be a werewolf?

Ethan Garraint is an old soul. He has been alive for hundreds of years, battling countless challenges and foes along the way— not the least of which was living through the genocide of the Cathar people at Montsegur, a society that wholly embraced him despite his lycanthropic nature. But in Volume 2 of The Clandestine Exploits of a Werewolf, he faces a dilemma that brings his past and present full circle, merging them both.

The Lady in the Blue Dress
6 x 9 Softcover & Hardcover 214 pages
ISBN 978-1-61342-600-5
ISBN (Hardcover) 978-1-61342-418-6

When she was a child, Mika Devalieur was introduced to her grandmother's most precious possession—a priceless and mysterious painting that she simply called The Lady in the Blue Dress. Upon Adele St. Clair's death, the painting is left in the care of her granddaughter with only one stipulation. Mika must hand over the family heirloom to a total stranger. Mika Devalieur desperately wants to deny her beloved grandmother's last request, but she can't. Torn between her Gran's last wishes and her desire to hold onto the Lady, she ultimately journeys to rural Virginia, where an enigmatic man shows her that this painting is only the beginning.

What quickly becomes clear is that James Clairmont knows much more about her and the Lady than he is letting on. He begins to slowly unravel a powerful supernatural connection that spans three generations of her family. Mika finds herself desperate to uncover the entire truth before she falls in love with a man filled with so many secrets—secrets about him, about her, and most especially about The Lady in the Blue Dress. (First published on Kindle Vella, episodes 1-23.)

Dumaine Street
6 x 9 Softcover & Hardcover 306 pages
ISBN 978-1-61342-902-0
ISBN (Hardcover) 978-1-61342-416-2

Voices in her head, catastrophic emotions, hallucinations—Rebecca Wells is more than convinced that she is losing her mind. And as a last-ditch effort, she contacts a self-professed counselor who seems convinced he can help.

Gabriel Sutton has abandoned the world of medicine to navigate a realm filled with psychic phenomena. Diagnosing Becca with extreme empathic abilities, he struggles to help her stabilize her gifts while trying desperately not to fall in love with his patient.

From the realm of vulnerability into a crusade to use their profound gifts to rescue others from peril on the other side of death, these two follow an astonishing and unpredictable path into each other's hearts.

The Tethering
A Portent of Crows
6 x 9 Softcover & Hardcover 201 pages
ISBN 978-1-61342-599-2
ISBN (Hardcover) 978-1-61342-419-3

Deborah Brandt's beloved Aunt Gena always told her that she was special, a bit different, and would have to live her life, unlike other people. Of course, this she disregarded as the ramblings of her lovely but notably eccentric aunt. Although there were the things that Aunt Gena said that seemed true—like Deborah being sensitive to energy shifts, having potentially psychic impressions, and dreaming of a spirit guide—none of it could be real. But the most ridiculous thing that her Aunt Gena told her before she died was that someone special was out there for her. She said that he was an extraordinary man who was not only her perfect match but someone who she would learn from so that they could help the world in difficult times. How ridiculous! It sounds like a fairy tale, and no such person exists.

Daniel Wren is unique. He has been raised and trained from a young age to hone his psychic gifts. He lives in a world unimagined by most. And he has been waiting for years to contact his counterpart, soulmate, if you will. But the problem is that she is painfully unaware of the type of life that he lives and the life she would be entering into if they came together.

His dilemma becomes how best to proceed. How can he win her over and move forward before outside forces take that decision away from him?

Travels into the Breach
Accounts of a Reluctant Mystic
6 x 9 Softcover & Hardcover 171 pages
ISBN 978-1-61342-323-3
ISBN (Hardcover) 978-1-61342-417-9

At first glance, his life seems quiet, serene, and even uneventful. Malachi McKellan, a 65-year-old widower and author of esoteric books, lives largely as a recluse in a house situated just off the banks of Bayou St. John in New Orleans. But unbeknownst to most, he is also a bit of a detective, a specific kind of detective whose specialty is psychic attacks. Alongside his lifelong companion and spirit guide Simon Tull, a 19th-century, 20-something English gent, Malachi battles the unseen, and is an unacknowledged hero to the most vulnerable. Most of the population have no idea what is really happening beneath the surface of the world in which they live.

In this collection of adventures, Malachi McKellan and Simon Tull wage war against the most insidious elements of the paranormal. In *The Three*, Malachi and Simon come to the aid of a young woman being victimized by a group of dark witches. An old apartment building is the scene of an unimaginable battle against monstrous forces in *The Lost Soul*. Malachi and Simon find themselves strategizing against a psychic vampire in *Obsession*, and *The Hotel* turns back time to the 1980s where Malachi confronts a demonic spirit. In *Between*, a past life is revisited as Malachi attempts to rescue a beloved sister from committing her existence to vengeance, and *The Wedding* takes a personal turn when Malachi must confront painful truths while endeavoring to protect his niece from a potentially devastating union.

Travel into the breach with a pair of paranormal warriors who choose to confront overwhelming forces on a battlefield unsuspected by most.

Gravier's Bookshop
A New Orleans Paranormal Mystery (#1)
6 x 9 Softcover & Hardcover 176 pages
ISBN 978-1-61342-288-5
ISBN (Hardcover) 978-1-61342-411-7

Max Gravier had no intention of becoming a recluse, but after his wife's death it seems his life is heading in that direction. He spends his time running Gravier's Bookshop on Magazine Street and occasionally on the quiet helps the police solve a crime with his psychic sensitivities. That is until he answers Caroline Breslin's call, a cry for help out of his dreams that draws him into a fierce battle for a young woman's soul.

In this first installment of The New Orleans Paranormal Mystery series, Caroline Breslin, an amazingly gifted empath, is determined to strike out on her own and has moved out from the protection of her family home. All is going extremely well until, of course, she comes under siege from a devastating supernatural attack. The last thing Caroline wants is to run back to her family for help, even though she is painfully in over her head.

What she really needs is a knight in shining armor—or maybe just that guy that keeps haunting her dreams.

Join them and the whole Breslin family psychic clan in this first installment of The New Orleans Paranormal Mystery Series where you'll travel into a new world just a few steps into the turbulent realm of the unseen.

The Hotel Mandolin
A New Orleans Paranormal Mystery (#2)
6 x 9 Softcover & Hardcover 146 pages
ISBN 978-1-61342-290-8
ISBN (Hardcover) 978-1-61342-412-4

Peril is wrapped up in the most enticing of disguises in *The Hotel Mandolin*, the second installment of The New Orleans Paranormal Mystery series. It's opulent, classic, and one of the most renowned hotels nestled deep in New Orleans' famous business district, but something is amiss at The Hotel Mandolin.

PI Peter Norfleet is calling out the big guns to help him investigate a recent suicide at the famous establishment—his good friend Max Gravier, a formidable psychic, and his girlfriend, Caroline Breslin, a talented empath. But none of them can seem to scratch the surface of this puzzle, no one except Cassie Breslin, Caroline's clairvoyant mother, who has somehow tapped into an unexpected connection with a tragic ghost from the turn of the century. And the more she uncovers, the more dangerous and malevolent the mystery becomes

More Books by Evelyn Klebert

The House at Pritchard Place
A New Orleans Paranormal Mystery (#3)
6 x 9 Softcover & Hardcover 138 pages
ISBN 978-1-61342-292-2
ISBN (Hardcover) 978-1-61342-413-1

Nothing is really wrong with the old Warrick House on Dante St. except that there most certainly is. Nothing is exactly wrong with its new mysterious owner except that Elise is sure that something doesn't add up. It isn't obvious, but sometimes the most dangerous things aren't.

In the third installment of The New Orleans Paranormal Mystery series, with the help of her very psychic sister and her children, the Breslin clan, Elise Ashford is about to embark on a wild rescue mission straight into another dimension that will land her squarely somewhere she doesn't expect, right back into her past. She'll land full circle; in a childhood home whose memory still haunts her to this day -- *The House at Pritchard Place.*

Treading on Borrowed Time
6 x 9 Softcover & Hardcover 223 pages
ISBN 978-1-61342-214-4
ISBN (Hardcover) 978-1-61342-436-0

For Julia Moreau, life seems complicated. Emerging from a failed marriage and managing a lifetime of diabetes, she lives alone in her childhood home where she communicates with the spirit of her Great Aunt Lilia. But Julia doesn't have a clue what complicated is until she is thrust into being the key chess piece in a match between two powerful men of extraordinary abilities on the wild hunt for a mystical creature hidden in the heart of New Orleans' French Quarter. Will Julia lose her soul to the karma of a devastating past life or her heart to the love of a man driven by dark forces? What is clear is that whichever way she turns she is *Treading on Borrowed Time.*

Sanctuary of Echoes
6 x 9 Softcover & Hardcover 371 pages
ISBN 978-1-61342-211-3
ISBN (Hardcover) 978-1-61342-409-4

Ghosts unacknowledged do not sleep.

Corey Knight has resigned herself to a quiet, reclusive life spent living out the rest of her days in her childhood home on the fringes of New Orleans' French Quarter. But the unexpected specter of her deceased father plunges her into a mad quest for a missing supernatural weapon unearthed long ago. And unfortunately, her only ally is a lost love she once betrayed.

Iain Shaw returns to New Orleans, a city he abandoned a decade before while fleeing a devastating past. Here, he is forced to confront it again in the visage of the woman he once adored - one that he is now determined to get back at any cost.

Follow them both in a wild paranormal tale of discovery and redemption as they confront and unearth the echoes of a buried and unyielding truth that once tore them irreparably apart.

A Quiet Moment
6 x 9 Softcover & Hardcover 273 pages
ISBN 978-1-61342-326-4
ISBN (Hardcover) 978-1-61342-435-3

Jacob Wyss is caught in a rut, in fact on the verge of being engulfed by it. After an excruciating and disillusioning divorce, his life as an artist in a sleepy-college town at the foot of the Appalachian Mountains has become quiet, routine, and maddening in its predictability. One wintry day, his deep restlessness drives him out in precarious conditions to a largely empty bookstore nearly devoid of another living soul, nearly.

Aimee Marston isn't like everyone else. On the surface, she lives a sedate life working as a feature writer for a small local newspaper in addition to several other editorial jobs to help make ends meet. But just beneath, her existence is largely not her own. She is a sensitive, an empathetic psychic, guided by her calling to use her gifts to help others. Unfortunately, as a result, her secretiveness has made her defensive, protective of herself, and prevented her from having much of a life.

A psychic call for help sends Aimee out on a freezing January morning where her destiny and Jacob's collide sending both their lives spiraling onto an unexpected and often disturbing track. Two lonely souls connect, not by accident, but by design. Theirs is the intersection of two spiritual paths, two lovers who must struggle to overcome the phantoms of a past life, as well as the challenges of their own inner demons to carve out an extraordinary future together.

A Ghost of a Chance
6 x 9 Softcover & Hardcover 230 pages
ISBN 978-1-61342-162-8
ISBN (Hardcover) 978-1-61342-440-7

You never know what's coming next.

Jack Brennan, an ambitious high-powered attorney, dies. But that's not the end, rather only the beginning. He finds himself constrained to an inexplicable afterlife as an earth-bound spirit trapped in an old Virginia farmhouse. His only companion is a very much living, reclusive writer of campy vampire novels. The maddening problem is that Hallie does not know he is there, nor that he is somewhat reluctantly falling in love with her.

Hallie Barkly is recovering from a painful and disillusioning divorce. Out of the ashes of her former life, she has managed to somehow forge a career and exorcise her demons by writing under the pseudonym of Sebastian Winters. Slowly, she is awakening to the fact that she is not alone.

Their lives intersect, and two unconventional lovers are brought together under insurmountable circumstances. Together they must battle an unseen force hell-bent on possessing Hallie's life and bridge death itself to make possible what cannot be—to find a chance.

Dragonflies - Journeys into the Paranormal
6 x 9 Softcover & Hardcover 176 pages
ISBN 978-1-88756-072-6
ISBN (Hardcover) 979-8-32548-418-6

In every form of creation, there is a blueprint for living, for experience, for interpretation. In flight, they can twist, turn, alter direction, pause in midair, and even fly backward. The dragonfly is the master of adaptability. They are a living prism, refracting light, and color, seemingly shifting their essence.

The lesson the dragonfly gives is that life is never what it appears to be.

In "The Wizard," as a novice practitioner of magic, Aurora Finn finds herself battling against the illusions of a powerful wizard intent on separating her from the world she knows. "The Sojourners" is a gentle story of a mother and daughter whose tenancy in an old Virginia farmhouse uncovers the trials and sorrows of its former occupants. A bookstore clerk gets an extraordinary customer on Halloween night in "Late One Night at Berstrums Books." In "The Tear," a woman coping with her fatal illness unknowingly begins a track on a mystical journey that will entirely restructure her vision of the world.

These stories follow the path of the dragonfly imbued with the momentum and energy of change, taking a winding and treacherous journey that ultimately leads to truth buried beneath perception.

Breaking Through the Pale
6 x 9 Softcover 134 pages
ISBN 978-1-88756-045-0

Journey with metaphysical author Evelyn Klebert into a collection of short stories that travel beyond the pale into the unpredictable realm of the paranormal.

In "A Grey Mourning," a disillusioned man encounters a mysterious being on the foggy streets of New Orleans. "Contact" is a tale of automatic writing, when a young artist establishes communication with a spirit guide, and the victim of a car crash unravels the true nature of her existence in "Dancing on the Threshold." The final tale is called "Isolation," in which a confused and disoriented woman finds herself in an old, quaint house where she must piece together the mystical implications surrounding her predicament.

The Witches' Own
6 x 9 Softcover & Hardcover 140 pages
ISBN 978-1-61342-058-4
ISBN (Hardcover) 978-1-61342-428-5

On the surface things seem quiet and serene in the picturesque coastal village of Kilmarnock, Virginia. But something unseen roams its lush forests as the past and present collide and the unthinkable begins to wreak its vengeance. Young Lucy Bonner is executed for witchcraft in the town's distant and brutal past. Her death triggers an unholy chain of events which grasp at the restless heart of novelist Peter McQuade, spurring him towards a quest to uncover the dark and terrifying truth.

More Books by Evelyn Klebert

The Left Palm
And Other Halloween Tales of the Supernatural
6 x 9 Softcover & Hardcover 122 pages
ISBN 978-1-93493-556-9
ISBN (Hardcover) 978-1-61342-442-1

Halloween is the time of year when that veil between worlds is thinned, and you can just catch a quick glimpse into the realm of the unknowable. In this collection of short stories, Evelyn Klebert takes you to a place where ordinary life splinters into the sphere of the paranormal.

The journey begins with one woman's unstoppable quest for vengeance against a supernatural creature in "Wolves" and continues in an old historical graveyard where a horrifying discovery is uncovered in "Emma Fallon." In "The Soul Shredder," a psychiatrist's unusual patient opens his eyes to a disturbing new view of reality, while in "Wildflowers," a woman strikes up a supernatural friendship with impossible implications. And in "The Left Palm," a fortuneteller in the French Quarter receives a most unexpected and terrifying customer.

White Harbor Road
And Other Tales of Paranormal Romance
6 x 9 Softcover & Hardcover 152 pages
ISBN 978-1-61342-066-9
ISBN (Hardcover) 978-1-61342-441-4

A psychic soul mate, a time traveler, a horror writer, and an enigmatic stranger take a selection of resilient, life-battered heroines to a place of paranormal healing and transformation. In this collection of short stories, *White Harbor Road* is the last stop where life's burdens and hardships evolve into something unexpected.

More Books by Evelyn Klebert

Explanations
6 x 9 Softcover 82 pages
ISBN 978-1-93493-515-6

In this, her second poetry collection, Evelyn Klebert takes us down the intricate path of a personal journey. Life with its particular struggles, pitfalls, and ultimately triumphs clearly begins to mirror a universal path, the quest for answers that we all ultimately pursue. In this reflective, esoteric collection we can all explore and seek some of life's elemental mysteries and hopefully when all is said and done emerge with some *Explanations*.

Considerations
6 x 9 Softcover 84 pages
ISBN 978-1-88756-062-7

Sometimes the struggle to understand the meaning and complexities of living comes down to a single moment of introspection or a fleeting yet meaningful reflection. This collection of poetry by Evelyn Klebert takes you down a winding path of self-discovery where the resolution may not always be absolute, but the journey is indeed unforgettable. It a wide and varied map of inspired poetry for your examination and consideration.

More Books by Evelyn Klebert

Appointment with the Unknown
The Hotel Stories
6 x 9 Softcover & Hardcover 155 pages
ISBN 978-1-61342-360-8
ISBN (Hardcover) 978-1-61342-421-6

A hotel, for most, represents a normal place, a predictable realm of commonality. One might even go as far to say a safe space, the reliable where nothing particularly unusual is expected to happen. Or is it? Dimensional traveling, spirit guides, mystical storms, and soul mates separated by time are only a few elements dotting this supernatural landscape. Drop into a collection of romantic paranormal stories where that place of commonality is only the threshold, the jumping-off point, for extraordinary adventures into the unknown.

Visit Evelyn's website at:
www.evelynklebert.com

Cornerstone Book Publishers
www.cornerstonepublishers.com

www.ingramcontent.com/pod-product-compliance
Lightning Source LLC
Chambersburg PA
CBHW010838250626
47157CB00011B/3311